HELLCAT BOOK 2

BLOOD ON THE TRACKS

WITHDRAWN

WILLIAM VITKA

A PERMUTED PRESS BOOK

ISBN: 978-1-68261-221-7
ISBN (eBook): 978-1-68261-222-4

Blood on the Tracks
Hellcat Book Two
© 2016 by William Vitka
All Rights Reserved

Cover art by Christian Bentulan

PERMUTED
PRESS

Permuted Press, LLC
permutedpress.com

Published in the United States of America

Also by William Vitka

The Hroza Connection series
Stranded
Emergence
Live, from the End of the World
A Man and His Robot
Blood God
Kill Machine

Bartender series
Bartender
Hitman
Godless

Hellcat series
Nightmare Highway
Blood on the Tracks
Book Three: New Eden coming soon

1.

Athena grabs the bitch by the throat. This chick who ~~tried to~~ sneak up on her. Pushes her fingertips into the veins and ~~arteries~~ there. Around the windpipe.

When the woman—this other competing scavenger—struggles, Athena drives a metal knee into her gut. Knocks the air outta the bitch and cracks the floating ribs. Then moves her hands to the back of the woman's head. Smashes the woman's face against the corner of a countertop that hasn't been used in fifteen years.

A doctor like Mark might say the temporal bone of the woman's head was broken. Maybe some other shit. But the female bleeds a lot. And her now-dead eyes bulge out. And that's what Athena wanted.

So Athena's happy about it.

Here in a rundown suburb of Columbus.

Where she had the bad luck of stumbling into three other scavengers. Two women and a man.

Now one woman and a man.

Parasites. Just like the survivors of Frankie. Just trying to collect what they can and hit the road.

But their presence here means Athena has to fight em. Not talk. Not hope for a peaceful resolution.

Forget the idea of morality. Kill and scavenge.

You own what you come across here.

Everyone else is an interloper.

A threat.

Athena ducks against the cabinets and the counter she just busted a woman's head on. Peers out dirty windows to try and get a grip on where the others might be. That man and woman.

Seems quiet. At least in part cuz Mark and Michelle are watching over the Hellcat a few blocks away. Them and the machine tucked inside a garage. So Athena doesn't have to contend with any of their whining.

She stays low. Reaches out for the body of her victim. Does a quick pat down of the corpse's clothes. Tattered leather jacket and cotton pants pockets. Only thing useful there is a pair of brass knuckles. Which Athena pilfers for herself and slides onto her right hand.

Athena peers out those dirty windows again. What'd be best is if those other two suckers would show themselves so she could let Mark and Michelle off their leashes and root around for supplies while she provides overwatch. That instead of this cat and mouse shit.

She creeps outside. Keeps her back to the pale orange siding of a tiny one-story house near the corner of Grasmere and East Como Avenues in North Linden. She's hidden by a front lawn that's a forest of dying grass and weeds.

The utter mess of a yard along the side of the house—gravel, decaying lawn chairs, several grills, what used to be a fridge, the fat battery-shaped container for some boozy energy drink called *Sparks* that she barely remembers, several truck skeletons—helps her hide as well.

She creeps. Creeps.

Boots making only the slightest *crunch.*

Athena catches a glimpse of movement farther down Como Avenue. The other side of the street. Two shapes. Male and female. They check the rusted husks of a Chrysler and a Buick, respectively.

The Hellcat driver moves along the side of a boat that probably ain't ever seen much water. Gets close to the street. Waits to make sure the man and woman ain't looking. Or they're at least distracted. Then throws herself over the pavement. Tucking. Rolling till she comes to a stop next to a dilapidated white single-car garage.

She waits again for any sign that the man or woman noticed her. Perks her ears up. Hears nothing. Edges up to the corner of the shabby garage. Peeks around the corner to eyeball her targets.

The man's still there. Half his body under the hood of the Buick. The woman walks off to the right toward the house. They're both dressed like road runners. Patched leather and boots. Which makes sense if they're digging around for supplies. But it doesn't make em friends.

Athena balls her fists. Steps out. Stalks like a cat. Slow. With bloody purpose. The brutal ridges of the brass knuckles pointed at the back of the man's head. A solid hit'll put the guy down. Then she can break his neck with the Buick hood or just leave him.

Safer to break his neck, though.

Unfinished business tends to follow you.

Which's really a bitch.

Athena feels a hammer blow to her back. Then her right shoulder. She stumbles forward. Stomps a boot heel down like an emergency brake. Her robotic right leg acts as a piston. Totally prevents any more forward movement. Allows her to pivot back and clothesline this second woman who's swinging a length of pipe.

The Hellcat driver's forearm digs right underneath the woman's chin. Collides with her throat. The force of Athena's attack flips the chick over. Causes her to drop the pipe. It *clangs* away on gravel thick enough to keep the weeds down.

Athena raises her right boot to stomp the woman's face in. Crush the skull and end that part of the fight.

Except the woman's cocksucker partner body-checks Athena and the best the Hellcat driver can do is roll and try to get her lungs fulla air again.

She doesn't stay down for more than a heartbeat. She turns. Faces the bastard.

He runs toward Athena. The pipe the bitch dropped raised above his head.

Athena lunges in kind. Shoulder low like a linebacker. She catches the cocksucker around the waist before he can make use of the pipe. Lifts him through adrenaline and willpower. Body slams him against the ground.

Before she can stand, she's parrying wild swing after wild swing from the bitch who's back on her feet.

Athena sees an opening. Snaps a quick, brass-knuckled jab into the woman's solar plexus. Not a lotta power. Just enough to stun and stagger the chick.

Which gives Athena the chance to stand. Pound the bitch's throat with a fist. Kick her hard in the gut so she wobbles backward toward the car husks. Doubles over. Pukes out stringy bile.

Athena turns back to catch the cocksucker again. He charges. Swings the pipe from the side this time. A post-apocalyptic baseball player.

She blocks his homerun hit at the wrists. Headbutts him. Cracks his nose. Blood flows in rivulets. She wrenches the pipe away. Knocks him upside the head with it. Pivots. Breaks the bitch's skull open. Hits her again. Till the chick lays still. Body in a heap.

The man scuttles back. Kicks and moves with his feet and elbows. Then stops.

Athena plods toward him. Twirls the pipe.

The man doesn't squeal or hold up a hand in defense.

What he does is unzip his jacket. Pull the dirty layers of shirts up to expose his chest.

The tattoo there.

A cross made from wrenches with a skull at the center.

The symbol of the Iron Cross loons.

The man smiles. Opens his mouth to say something.

Athena doesn't let him talk. She slams the pipe down into his open gullet.

The man's eyes go wide.

She pushes the pipe farther. Till he chokes and blood bubbles up around the metal.

Athena grunts.

Thinks of her mantra: *I am strong. I am death. I am the absence of forgiveness. There is no poetry for me, for I am that. Strength. Death. The absence of forgiveness.*

Then again, these Iron Cross assholes seem to be the "absence of forgiveness" as well.

Athena grunts again.

* * *

The dust of the edge of the Midwest settles around Athena's boots. Innumerable skin flakes from the dried out husk of the American Dream.

She grinds out the smoldering butt of her last cigarette with a heavy heel. Into the dirt and gravel at the side of the road.

Thinks: *Shit*.

Of all the supplies she didn't wanna run out of, smokes were right at the top.

Her own damn fault, though. Mindlessly chain smoking ever since they left Frankie's fucked up funhouse in Perry, Ohio.

She wants a solid view of the Columbus cityscape from the suburbs but can't find one anywhere along I-71. Whole place is too fuckin flat. This amoebic spread of suburbia that surrounds a city dead before its time.

Smoke. She sees a singular pillar of smoke and that's about it.

Well, aside from the dog-sized bugs that randomly appear at the edges of her purview before scuttling back into the weeds that're like forests for merry bandits to hide in.

The insects don't seem to care much about her or Mark or Michelle. Not yet, anyway. The biggest threat from em they've encountered was a grasshopper big as a Great Dane—and even then, it was only cuz the fucker might've totaled the Hellcat.

Crazy green bastard hopping across the road.

Regardless, they ain't even into the wastes yet. Not the *real* wastes. The cursed lands cursed further by assholes in bars where the booze remains more trustworthy than the water or the customers.

Athena bites her lips. They're in another section of North Linden. A ways up the road from Columbus by five or so miles.

They've been scavenging. Regaining all the bits and pieces that make survival a possibility instead of a wish:

Drinkable water. Canned food. Toilet paper. Ammo—.45-caliber for Athena's 1911 and 12-gauge for the replacement sawed-off double-barrel. Diapers for Michelle's incoming baby. Powdered milk, if they're lucky. Rare items like chapstick. Vaseline. Lotion that can be traded for gas. Fuel.

Or, hell, eggs. Butter. Shortening to make cookies.

Those sweets were the best bargaining tool Athena ever had.

Not that the little Easy-Bake Oven in her trunk is gonna get much use with all her supplies gone.

Athena watches the brother-sister duo, Mark and Michelle, trundle out the front door of a nearby beige house. Might be the sixtieth or seventieth place they've hit on their route to Columbus.

Her hand hovers as always over the butt of her 1911.

Mark's hands hold a few tins of food. And there's a soft-looking blanket over his shoulder.

Michelle's hands hold a basket of interwoven wood. Inside Athena sees baby powder. A tube of toothpaste. Something that looks like Neosporin. A few loose rounds of ammo whose calibers are unknown.

It's a good haul, all told.

Especially for the suburbs.

Athena nods. Watches as the two siblings move their ill-gotten gains to the Hellcat.

The brother and sister don't say anything in return.

All three know each other better than that by now.

And Athena still eyes the three as commodities.

The brother, as a doctor.

The sister, as a viable woman.

The soon-to-be baby, as worthy of trade.
The madness of Frankie's compound did not soften Athena.
Her goal remains the same: Get to California.
And die her own way.

2.

Ain't till 71 offers em a split off onto 670, toward Dayton, that Athena finds a good view of Columbus. Even then, it ain't till she can get clear of the dark brown retaining walls of the highway.

Athena uses the one working lens on a busted pair of binoculars to scan the skyline from left to right. The cracked skeletons of Ohioan architecture claw up at the sky.

She doesn't know any of the building names. Doesn't care much, either. Only reason they're in Columbus at all is the radio station that's still cranking out a signal. A twenty-four-hour show run by two brothers.

The hope is to get as much info as they can before they continue west. Trade for fuel. Ask about a map of possible gas dump locations—Athena's thinking being that if these two suckers are still on the air, they gotta know where a steady supply of gas is. The juice to run generators for their station.

Michelle mutters from the passenger side of the car. Over the hood. Hand on her belly. "How are we gonna find the radio station where they're broadcasting from?"

Athena grunts. "Wherever the two brothers are? Dapper. . . Dapper? Dapper fuckin Don and Dan." She shakes her head. Horrible goddamn names. "Wherever those goobers are, there'll be lights at night. Electricity giving em away. I get the fuckin feeling—" she waves her hands around at the desolation. Random cars without occupants. "This ain't the liveliest place."

Mark snorts in the backseat. "Columbus never was."

Athena looks in the rear window. Frowns at him. The brother still hurting from Frankie's—like they all are. "Columbus still got *some* life left. Better than most of the country can say. Right now." She looks back to the skyline. The smoke. The invisible radio signal pumping from. . .somewhere. "Being able to hear ZZ Top? Shit, even the Eagles, and I hate the fuckin Eagles. Ain't bad."

She shrugs. "All things considered."

Memories of Frankie nowhere near gone as they oughtta be.

All things considered.

Athena eases into the driver's seat. Michelle into the passenger's.

The Hellcat growls and prowls along the 670 West offramp. The engine cycles down as Athena lets her foot off the gas. She and her machine grumble along the cracked asphalt. Baking blacktop. Titanic weeds and grass pushed back by obvious motor traffic.

They'd heard engines on the way to Columbus. Never stopped though.

Athena figured the other drivers were as wary as she was.

No reason to get into a fight.

Better to limp ahead on amputated limbs than lose everything.

Right?

Sure.

Sure.

Athena grimaces. The metal limb—whatever Mark did in the surgical bay—that comprises her right leg works fine. But she can't stop thinking about it. This machinery that she scratches at when phantom itches worm their way into her brain. She expects to find flesh. Instead, there's chrome. An articulated knee and articulated ankle.

She wonders. Worries.

The leg and the chrome. Wired into her body. She's probably the new owner of a fiend limb. The same android shit that powered Frankie's freaky minions. And what powered *them?* A battery. Some form of electricity she and the Iron Cross goons were able to ruin and thereby ruin the fiends.

So what's powering Athena's new leg? The juice her own body generates? A battery hidden in the metal thigh or calf?

Worse: Is it possible that her new leg could rebel against her? Poison her? Shut down her heart or other vital organs?

Go rogue?

Athena sniffs. Slaloms the Hellcat between a couple of random wrecks toward exit 4B off 670. That puts em on US-23 South.

The road curves into the heart of Columbus. On the left yawns a monstrous parking lot. On the right is the remains of the city's convention center. Most the signage letters still intact. Its grey concrete walls painted over haphazardly in rainbows of colors with pleas for help. Food. Water. Military assistance.

The germ that was killed by her cancer and others', the germ that killed everyone *without* cancer, she figured it hit everyone at the same time. Made the whole country die at once. Maybe not. Maybe the people out here suffered. Or maybe the survivors just *hoped* there was a rescue worth waiting for.

A brick and beige hotel sits near the highway. Most of the windows are blown out.

Athena traces lines of rope from the upper floors. Skeletons dangle at the ends. Nooses around their neck bones. The tattered remains of clothing like sad flags in a lackluster breeze.

Mark and Michelle are silent.

Athena sees their eyes, though. Eyes that bounce around and tally the human toll the emptiness tells of. The abandon.

They take it slow.

Aging brick buildings with white paint that falls away. A tall advertisement from Ohio State University that reads: "There is no routine cancer."

Farther along, more big parking lots. Largely empty. Whatever vehicles had been there no doubt stolen away for scrap use elsewhere. A mix of high-end residential—glass covered cubes for living. Enormous Renaissance hotel tower. Across the street is a "Law & Finance" building with a brass front.

The green grounds of the Ohio Statehouse have, of course, erupted with plants. The whole building encased in the embrace of wild vines.

Only thing Athena can say for sure about Columbus is that is does seem totally goddamn devoid of human life. She hasn't spotted any traps—obvious ones, anyway. Nobody's come out to greet em or attack em. There ain't even any signs of inhabitants.

The radio—tuned to 96 FM, same station Michelle found the Dan and Don brothers on—cranks out a steady stream of rock staples. Right now it's Crosby, Stills & Nash doing "Suite: Judy Blue Eyes." A song Athena's never had much affinity for. The name being just so fuckin clever.

Point is: The Dapper brothers themselves haven't made a peep since Don came on in the morning, when the Hellcat crew were fleeing Frankie's. About seven hours ago. The hundred-eighty mile trip from the Perry nuke plant taking more than twice what it should, since they had to do so much scavenging.

Could be, there ain't no news and no reason to go on-air.

Could be, the brothers are too busy watching the Hellcat.

This new muscle car-interloper in their midst.

Athena hangs a right at a big, weather-beaten sign for "COLUMBUS COMMONS PARKING." She makes the first left she can into the multi-level, empty concrete garage. Ignores the "Exit Only" warnings. Blows passed the ticket-payment machines, their wooden arms long-since destroyed. She winds the Hellcat up up up to the roof. Five floors above ground level.

Michelle scrunches her face. Says, "What're we doing?"

Athena shuts down the Hellcat. "Getting off the street. Getting a better view." She snaps her fingers at Mark. "Radio."

He grabs the little hand-crank electronic. Offers it to Michelle outside. His sister sets about monitoring 96 FM. He himself follows Athena to the northeast corner of the roof. The road runner's got her busted pair of binoculars. She peers through the one working lens.

Mark winces as he rests his elbows on the concrete ledge. "Seems quiet."

Athena sighs. "As the cliché goes, that's what worries me."

He looks her over. Waits a second. "You aren't smoking."

Athena sneers at him. "None left. Not that it should concern you." She growls. "You're here out of a basic need."

"And I guess *basic* healthcare isn't part of that."

Athena grunts. Yeah, Mark probably saved her with that surgery at Frankie's. But that doesn't mean she has to enjoy being part cyborg. Part *fiend*.

She catches a glint of light from the roof of a light brown building to their north. Knows it's the sun reflecting off glass. Some visual aid like hers.

Athena throws herself against the pavement of the roof. She tucks up against the concrete wall. Takes instinctive cover in case that flash, that glint, is a sniper scope.

Mark looks to her. Mouth curved down and a little open in dumb surprise.

She frowns at him. This idiot who doesn't know when to protect himself.

But he ain't been shot yet.

There is that.

She can accept him being a target.

Athena waits a heartbeat.

Cocks an eyebrow at the yet-unshot Mark.

Okay.

Not a sniper then.

Mark says, "What the hell are you doing?"

Athena stands. Goes back to the corner. Sticks the binoculars up against her face again. The glint hasn't moved. Now there's a motion behind it. A hand moving back and forth in a wave.

She frowns.

The music from the radio in Michelle's hands dies. Up fades a voice. The same sorta goofy, lilting radio voice from before:

"Dapper Don here. Sorry to cut that one short, road runners. But you and I know the truth: Bon Jovi marches on, dead or alive. And, well, what the *heck*! Why did I ruin that song? Looks like we've got a visitor here in our fair final beacon of light before the wasteland. Ah, wait, correction." There's the sound of a door opening. Papers being shuffled. Another, muffled voice. "Visi*tors.* Plural." He laughs. "Ho-*leee* crap, it's the *Hellcat* and her crew. Up and coming legends." The sound of a hand covering the microphone. More muffled voices. A pause. More muffled voices. A throat clearing.

Then, Dapper Don returns: "Hellcat, do yourself a favor a look west. I'll give you a moment before I go on."

Athena winces. She hates being identified. Located when she doesn't know exactly what the deal is. She hates even more that there might be some mean motherfuckers listening to these radio guys, learning where she is.

The disc jockeys have plenty to lose too, though.

So she raises the busted binoculars to her eyes anyway. Looks west. Between the buildings. Over the slow churning sludge of the Scioto River. The clusters of homes that make up the suburbs.

It takes her eyes a moment to distinguish the dirty brown wasteland from the swirling brown right above it.

A dust storm.

Athena groans.

The storm rises high into the sky. A hundreds foot-tall wall of particles that tumble and rumble like an earthen tidal wave.

Dapper Don says over the radio, "That storm'll clobber anything on the street. We get em once every few of days. Maybe once a week. Winds whip up all the dead, untended soil from the farmlands in the Midwest and hurl it our way. They usually peter out near the eastern city limits. But…if you wanna keep your machine in one piece, I suggest you roll north to our building.

"And do it before dark. That's when the muties come out to play with the bugs."

3.

The radio jockeys tell em to head up High Street. Make a right on East Chestnut. Stash the Dodge inside the big parking structure that's attached to their building. Either Dan or Don'll meet em at the elevated, covered walkway that leads from their tower to the garage.

Athena does what they suggest. Not cuz she trusts the two. Only cuz that dust storm might ruin everything.

She'd rather protect the car and die than lose the car and live.

Athena parks the Hellcat at an angle near the elevated walkway. Positions it so they can take cover behind the car if needed. She shuts the engine off. Sits in the driver's seat for a moment. Thinks. Waits.

She opens her door. Walks over to the trunk. Fishes out a second, large holster that she wraps snug around her left, still-human leg. Slips the sawed-off shotgun into that. She mentally tallies up the ammunition situation: three 12-gauge shells. Eleven .45 rounds.

Not good.

Probably enough to kill the two jockeys, but not good.

Athena wordlessly beckons Michelle and Mark to her side. A quick flip of her hand.

Two shapes appear in the tunnel to the garage. Both hobble. Limp.

Athena squints. Waits for the shapes to hit the doorway. Keeps her right hand over her Springfield 1911. Left over the sawed-off shotgun.

Dapper Don and Dan go from pausing, halting shadows to pausing, halting humans in a blink. They halt at the entrance. Offer shaky waves to Athena. Mark. Michelle. These two brothers. Hunched over. Both in ill-fitting jeans. Shirts. Sneakers. Smiling. Maybe twins. Both hit hard by similar birth defects: small size, spines bent with something like scoliosis, abnormalities in their faces. Lumps. Asymmetries in the extreme.

But still smiling regardless. Crooked jaws and ruined teeth and bright, eager eyes.

Mark sighs. Looks at em both with genuine concern.

Genuine sadness.

One of the brothers nods. The one on the right, in an oversized white Cleveland Indians jersey. "Yeah. How we look… Momma and poppa liked to drink." He blinks at the floor. "Other stuff too." Frowns. "Radiation hasn't helped. Haha!" He points his fingers at the group. Looks up again to Mark. Then Michelle. Athena. Offers a weaker smile than before. Seems to realize gallows humor works worse when the whole world's already hanging by the noose.

The brother on the left, in a black sweater, says, "Our brains are solid, though. Nothing wrong up there."

"When we were little, our poppa used to *scream* that we had *faces for radio*." The brother on the right spreads out two gnarled hands. Like he's waiting for the audience to laugh.

But they ain't.

Michelle's eyes water. She sniffs.

Athena knows the brunette is thinking about her own baby.

The brother on the right gives em another second. Groans. "I've wanted to tell that joke for a while, but I guess it's too depressing, all things considered."

The brother in black rests a hand on his kin's shoulder. Does a brief introduction. Points to his dark sweater. Says, "I'm Dapper Dan." He pats his brother. "This is Dapper Don."

Don stares at the ground. Lifts a weary hand and waves.

Dan sniffs. "We're really glad to see you guys. I mean that. Y'know, jeez. The *Hellcat*." He chuckles. "*Here*, with us. That's gonna be good radio."

Athena cracks her neck. Lets her hands float away from the weapons at her sides. These two are like children. A touch deranged. Deformed. But innocent in a strange way. "I ain't leaving my car here for some asshole to steal."

Don looks up finally. Smiles a sad smile. "Hellcat, there isn't anyone alive in Columbus *to* steal it."

* * *

Dan and Don lead the road-ravaged trio through the walkway. To a bank of elevators. One actually works, Dan says. Powered by solar panels on the roof.

He chuckles. "When everyone else dropped, and my brother and I found ourselves with lots of time on our hands, we learned how to maintain the electrical systems in this building. Thankfully, it wasn't in bad shape to begin with."

Don nods. "Plus the only wear and tear it gets is from us."

Athena grunts.

Mark scratches his cheek. "You're being literal when you say there's nobody else in Columbus."

Dan shrugs. "Only other human being is Crazy Mason, but he doesn't trust the elevator so he never comes up to the studio floor where we live."

The elevator light in the wall dings. A translucent plastic circle turns steady, illuminated white.

Michelle frowns. "Does. . .Crazy Mason have a good reason to distrust the elevator here?"

Don shakes his head. "No. I mean, we call him 'Crazy Mason' after all."

Athena squints. Shifts her weight from one foot to the other. Her hands return to their places near the butts of her guns.

Dan and Don smile in earnest.

Athena says, "You got smokes up there?"

Don nods. "I think we have a few cartons of Lucky Strikes from some road runners who passed through a while ago. We don't smoke." He smirks. "Enough health problems as it is, but they're useful to barter with." He gestures for the trio to squeeze into the elevator.

Athena leads. Mark and Michelle follow.

Athena says to the deformed kin, "And what do you want in return?"

Dan looks over his shoulder at her as he hits the button for the tenth floor. "We want an exclusive interview of course."

The doors close. Music from the radio station sounds from unseen speakers. Sounds like early Rolling Stones, but the volume's pretty low.

Don says, "And maybe some of those cookies?"

Athena grunts. "Only if you've got the raw goods. Eggs. Butter. Chocolate chips. . . ."

The elevator hums. Groans along its trek upward.

After a moment. Two. The doors open again.

Dan and Don step out. Each does a little bow and spreads his arms.

It's the first time Athena or Mark or Michelle have seen functioning lights in. . . .

It's been a long fuckin time since the trio of road runners have seen functional indoor lights that weren't cobbled together and running off some dinky generator.

Other than Frankie's.

Bright suns in the ceiling. On desks as decoration.

It seems like a waste to Athena.

But Mark and Michelle's jaws drop.

They remember being spoiled with childish glee.

Dan says, "Welcome to the former Q96-FM—"

Don says, "—and the current D96-FM."

The radio floor is covered in dark grey carpet. Grey walls. With black baseboards. The raggedy furniture at the entrance—a couple of armchairs with wood frames and fat black seating—is deep purple.

Which, Athena thinks, was probably someone's idea of a joke.

Not that she dislikes "Smoke on the Water."

None of this distracts from how amazingly maintained the

whole place is. Gorgeous. A relic of modern civilization before the germ.

There are still black and white photos of the deejays who came before Dan and Don on the wall. Portraits. Almost a shrine.

Michelle takes a step closer to inspect.

Dan doesn't intercept her, but he gets close. Stands right beside her. Starts to point. Excited to show off to this new guest. "Oh oh, that's Torg and Elliot. Man, they were great. And, heh—" Dan looks at his feet. "We always had a crush on Laura Palmer, but. . . ."

Mark watches with a smile.

Athena's face doesn't move. Her eyes bounce from Michelle to Dan to Mark to Don. A constant frown. Then the rest of her body follows. She turns. Jabs a finger at Don. "Where're the fuckin smokes."

Not a question.

Don flinches. Stammers. "J-Jesus, you're going to be a tough interview, aren't you." He hobbles down a hall. Opens the door to a studio apparently used to stockpile goods, cuz he returns with a carton of Lucky Strikes and hands it to Athena with a slightly bowed head.

She takes it. Tears it open. Rips into the first pack. Pulls a stogie free with her teeth. Lights it and immediately seems less angry.

Don lifts his eyebrows. "Wow, you were really fiending, huh? How long has it been since you had a cigarette? Days? Weeks?"

Athena sighs. "Couple hours."

Don blinks. Waits a heartbeat. Two. "Okay then."

Mark wanders by his sister and Dan, Dan still engaged in telling some of the station's history, and says to Don, "How do you guys keep all this running?"

Don snaps his fingers. "Ah." Smiles. "Very reasonable question." He starts off down the same hall again. Talks. "As strange or unlikely as it may seem, everything we have is from donations." He opens the door to the station's stockpile.

Athena sees cases of beer. Pens and paper. Toiletries. Baby wipes. Powdered milk. A heavy bin with a random assortment of ammo. A couple of rifles and shotguns—not in great shape, but probably functional. CDs. DVDs. Blu-rays. A few monitors. Televisions. There's also a fridge and a freezer. The contents of which might actually allow her to bake those cookies. . . .

She crosses her arms over her chest. "You're like PBS or something? People pay you to stay on the air?"

Don nods. "Sort of. When you're the only live radio station at the end of the world—" He chuckles. "What Dan and I do, it makes road runners out there feel a little better. At least, that's what they tell us when they come through."

Athena grunts. Smokes.

Don says, "It's kind of funny, that. Corporations tried so hard to kill radio off when there was still a civilization. Now it's one of the few things to survive our extinction." Don turns to Athena and Mark. "Can I get you guys some snacks? Water? I figure we'd save the big meal celebration for after the interview, but I can get everyone some munchies beforehand too."

Mark says, "Yeah, water would be great. And my sister needs to eat badly. Something healthy, though, for the baby."

"Okay, I can do that." Don looks to Athena. "And for you?"

"Whiskey."

"You don't, uh. . .don't want any food or—"

Athena scowls. "Just whiskey."

4.

Dan sits Athena down in their one operational radio studio. Her butt plops down into the black fabric of a swiveling office chair.

He walks around to the other side of the big desk at the center of the room. It all laid out with glowing buttons and lights and instruments to keep track of audio levels. He checks his headset. Fits it around his misshapen skull. Pulls his mounted microphone a bit closer to his lips.

Athena can hear the faint guitar chugs of ZZ Top coming through a small nearby speaker. The song is winding down. "La Grange." A classic.

Through the big window in the studio, she sees Mark and Michelle and Don outside. These grinning people. The three shoving food in their faces. Bottled water and Doritos. Cheetos.

What could this evening's glorious dinner be?

More random shit from a goddamn vending machine?

Dan points to Athena, then to his headset. Then to his microphone.

Athena sighs. Sets up her headset. Microphone. She notices the mic's thin little pop screen in front. Wonders if it'll actually keep her from bouncing into the red levels if she says her "P"s too hard.

As "La Grange" ends, Dan cues his microphone. Pushes a few buttons. Fades himself up into the fade-down of ZZ Top's guitar licks. "Hello road runners. Dapper Dan here. Hope you all enjoyed that 1973 classic from the Texas trio."

Despite his appearance, his voice is strong. Bold. Deep, but hitting the right notes.

To Athena, Dan sounds like Harry Shearer.

Not that this impresses her much.

She lights another cigarette.

Dan continues. "We have a pretty special guest for you all today. A name that's already being whispered across the wastes."

Athena has no idea if any of this is fuckin true, but she gets the shtick.

She smokes and tries to look comfortable. Even though she's anxious and doesn't want to talk.

Dan locks eyes with her. Leans toward the mic. Growls a little. "Though I have to say, you might have heard her big V8 before you heard *her*." He claps. "The one." Clap. "The only." Clap. "*Hellcat* is here in the D96 studio with us today." He hits a button on his side of the desk. Canned applause floats out to the airwaves.

Athena rolls her eyes.

Then again, she's never been a guest on a radio show, and as far as she knows, Dan and Don have never *had* a guest so. . .

Dan says, "Well, let's hear from the woman herself. Hellcat, what brings you to Columbus? And where are you from, anyway? You've got a legend building behind you. I think our listeners want to know more about you."

Athena breathes smoke. Dan becomes her long lost David for a blink. Then he's gone. She glances at her microphone. Cocks an eye. "I need fuel and resupply." She shrugs at Dan. Almost like she expects the listeners to hear her lack of interest in the question. Like her response is the most obvious thing in the fuckin world.

There's dead air for a second. Several seconds.

Dan bites his lips. Furrows his brow.

Dead air is a serious sin in radio.

Dan says, "I think everyone out there can appreciate your need to be laser-focused on getting done what needs getting done." He nods. "We want to know who the *real* Hellcat is." He pauses. "Like, where did you come from? What *is* the Hellcat story?"

Athena thinks: *This's getting to be a bit too fuckin daytime TV for my tastes.*

But then she remembers that these two goofballs are her best shot at getting restocked for the road ahead.

That's all that matters right now.

Plus, icing em on-air, live? If they really are beloved symbols of an America long-gone, then she'll be hunted. Or, at least, it'll make any future bartering real hard.

So she takes a deep breath. Gets ready to say more than she ever has to a single human being other than David.

And, worse, with a fuckin audience.

Athena says, "I'm from New York City. I was there, with my husband, when the germs hit fifteen years ago. I don't know what caused it. I don't know any more than anyone else.

"What I know is that the cancers we share ate up the germ before the germ could end us." She arches her eyebrows at nothing. Her feet. The darkness under the radio desk. "The only thing the *doctors* knew was that cancer was stronger." Athena takes a pull from her whiskey bottle. "That's uniquely fucked, huh? The religious extremists go after the States and their bug packs a punch, sure—" Athena chuckles. "But it can't beat good, old American cancer."

She takes another pull.

Breathes smoke.

"That's what I've heard, anyway." Athena shrugs. "Some extremist assholes got a hold of the right mix. Planted *Patient Zero's* on planes. Boats. All these biological time bombs aimed at the Western world." She shrugs again. "Does it matter?" She blinks. Cocks an eye at Dan. "I don't even know if they were even Muslims, in the end. Or nutty Zionists or nutty Christians. I'm just saying *someone* did this to us."

Dan nods. "As in, not an act of God. Or nature."

Athena snorts. "*Pft.* No. I don't buy any of that. I mean, sure, there's always gonna be some group of assholes who thinks it was 'God' or 'nature's intention' or whatever the fuck." She sits up in her chair. Adjusts her butt. "Davi—" She catches herself. "My husband and I spent a lotta time talking about it. Talking to others about it. We tried to piece the pieces together." She shakes her head. "The kind of kill-your-ass-dead lethality the germs had? Way too efficient. Way too human and results-oriented. Mother Nature ain't actually all that efficient. That's why evolution takes so long. It's all these little steps, right? Tiny, tiny steps in the right direction. But the germ? Bam. Then ninety percent of the planet is dead. That smacks of a designer germ."

"And, uh. . . ." Dan hums. "I want to get back to the germ at some point—your theories on it—but, you and your husband obviously survived the germ. Where is your husband now?"

Athena shifts. Smokes. Silence hangs in the air. Then she says, "Dead."

"I'm sorry to hear that."

"Yeah." Athena drinks. "Everybody's sorry." She casts a grim look out to Don and Mark and Michelle.

Dan presses a button that mutes his microphone as he coughs. Hacks. Spits some gooey matter into the trashcan near his feet. He comes back to the mic. Says, "So you've been driving all the way from New York City."

"Just outside, but yeah."

Dan spreads his hands. "So. . .where are you headed?"

"California."

"What's in California?"

Athena cocks an eye at Dan. "Peace and fuckin quiet."

Dan chuckles. "Okay." *Haha.* "Maybe a slightly touchy subject."

Athena thinks: *This whole thing's starting to feel goddamn touchy.*

Dan says, "What about Frankie? What happened there?" He looks over at some papers. "A short while before you arrived, we had two other visitors. Both claiming to be members of the Iron Cross." He looks back up at Athena. "They were in a pickup truck and they claimed that *you*—the Hellcat—killed Frankie and destroyed his facility up in Perry."

Athena nods. "I did."

She doesn't mention Frankie's assertion that he was working on a cure for cancer. Doesn't mention that Bullhorn's protégé, Sherlock, seemed pretty damn sure there'd be value in Frankie's research. . .right before she blew the whole fuckin facility to hell.

Nope. That can all sit in her head.

Dan says, "I think that's a major relief for everyone. Heck, I can see your legend growing just while you sit there." He smiles. "Can you tell our listeners what happened there?"

Athena frowns. "That ain't up for discussion."

She thinks about the nightmare. The fiends. The machines. Frankie's psychotic fixation on her. How he built all those mad things from flesh and metal. The obscene perversions he inflicted on her.

How she lost her goddamn motherfuckin *leg*.

"I think our listeners—"

"I think your listeners can eat a dick. All the dicks. I killed that fuckball Frankie and that's where this conversation ends." Athena stands. Drops her headset onto the desk. "I've done more talking in five minutes than I have in ten years."

Dan watches her from his seat. Wide-eyed. A little scared. He sniffs. Laughs into the microphone. "Well folks, there's the Hellcat for you! Living up to her reputation as one tough-talking, ass-kicking lady. I think we're going to let her get back to business before she cracks open my old head like a melon." He pauses. Hits a few buttons. "Here's REO Speedwagon to see you folks into the evening. 'Back on the Road Again' on D96-FM."

He kills his microphone. Hobbles toward Athena. Says, quietly, eyes down, "I didn't mean to upset you."

Athena grunts.

He says, "I was just trying to do. . .what they do on the radio. What they *used* to do. There was supposed to be a format to this stuff. I'm sorry."

Athena studies him. This meek little man. Sheepish. The two brothers so far being the only two decent human beings she's come across.

She sighs. "Don't be sorry." Puts a hand on his shoulder. "It's fine. We're good."

Dan locks eyes with her. "Are you sure?"

"I'm sure I'm sure."

Dan smiles. "Thank God. That's a load off my mind." He chuckles. Opens the studio door. Ushers Athena through.

Don and Mark and Michelle offer some light applause.

Mark says, "Sounded great. You're a *wonderful*, entertaining personality as long as you're at a distance."

Michelle says, "Yeah, it was kinda funny. Till the end."

Athena waves her off.

Don brings his hands together and rubs em. "So, who's hungry for a real meal?"

Athena cocks an eye. "Define 'real meal.'"

He dips his head. "Follow me." And leads the crew down another hall. This one farther from the lobby. To a door marked with crayon. It reads: GOOD EATING.

Don leans over. Digs a key on a chain from around his neck. Unlocks. Throws the door open. Crosses his arms and leans a little to show how pleased he is to show this off.

There are entire pallets of canned goods inside.

Don says, "We have delicacies. From the great chefs of America's Choice to Chef Boyardee and even Campbell's annnnd right to your mouths."

Dan joins em. "If you check the freezers, I think we have Stouffer's too." He grins. "I love those big fat macaroni and cheese tubs."

"And there's a microwave. Though it'd be better for our reserves if we set up some butane camping stoves under the cans and just cooked the food that way."

"Otherwise?" Dan gestures to the room. "Help yourselves."

Don smiles. "We rarely get guests we actually enjoy having around."

At this, Athena is immediately suspicious.

Who, exactly, has been visiting the two brothers. And would the brothers rat out Athena if the chance was there?

She can imagine the Iron Cross—if the gang is as expansive as Bullhorn suggested—putting a nice price on her fuckin head. Maybe use Mark as a slave doctor. Michelle as breeding stock.

Athena doesn't believe for a second that these two freaks are men of their word.

She keeps her distance. Doesn't get too cozy. Grabs a can of "Spaghetti & Meatballs," though she doubts there's anything so recognizable in the tin. Her voice is a low growl. "Thanks for the grub." She pops the can's top. Picks up a plastic spoon from one of the short tables. Digs in.

Between mouthfuls, she says, "We'll eat then be on our way. Just need to know where we can refuel."

Mark and Michelle watch her. Their lips flat lines. Eyes wide. Curious. They each have a can of Campbell's soup in their hands. "Hearty Chicken Noodle." Mark's near a camping stove. The butane deal Don mentioned. They're in no rush. But they know that what Athena says goes.

Very literally, her way *is* the highway.

Dan and Don stop. Their grins dip.

Don stammers. Again. "Y-you can't leave."

Athena slows her chewing. Sticks her spoon into the can. She pulls her .45 1911 with her right hand. Keeps it low, though. Doesn't aim. "Why."

"The-the-the storm. . . It will be here soon." Don looks like he's holding his breath.

Dan puts a hand up. "We told you about the storm. And when the storm comes, so do the bugs. And when the bugs come, the mutants come to feast."

"It's death on the streets. Chaos and madness. In the morning, it will all be gone again. Clean. The bugs and the mutants will pick it all clean, but—"

"But tonight, you can't go out. They will kill you and destroy your machine."

Mark and Michelle continue to watch. Still unsure if they should—or even *can*—heat up their soups.

Athena bites her lip. Thinks. Her eyes flit from Dan to Don to Mark to Michelle.

She holsters her pistol. Resumes eating. "At daybreak, then."

The brothers nod. Exhale.

Mark blinks. Gets back to the task of igniting the camping stove.

Michelle opens her mouth. The start of a sentence emerges. But she shuts it a heartbeat later.

Athena chews. Empties her can. Examines the stockpile. Wonders how much she can get away with taking before the brothers get antsy.

Outside, the winds pick up. The first particulates of the giant storm slap against the building. Random *pings* and *pangs*.

Metal groans and bends.

Athena thinks: *It's another illusion of safety.*

5.

The storm arrives with spectacular force. A howling maelstrom of dust and debris from the west. It makes its presence known with winds that carry dirt and scuttling insects. Winds that cry in the evening sky. Wail. Ghost-like.

And colors.

All these mad colors cast up in the air. Collisions of hues. Striking and oddly beautiful for the sheer fact that they don't belong together at all.

Red and rust of the dust shimmering against bright blue above. The sunset on Mars.

Athena squints into the evening gloom from the windows of an empty office on the tenth floor. A whirling brown dervish on its way from the west. Not all that different from the mess of Dinty Moore beef stew in the can she holds.

If she looks hard enough, she thinks she can catch the squirming forms of whatever insectoid nightmares are a-tumblin through the wind.

She inhales. Exhales. Plops the Dinty Moore can on a vacant desk. Crosses her arms. Lights a cigarette.

A voice behind her says, "It's kind of pretty, isn't it?"

Athena looks over her shoulder. Smoke trails. She nods to Don.

Don hobbles. Joins her side. He watches with her. Nods himself when a locust with a five-foot wingspan dives by the building. Membranous wings spread wide.

"What I remember," Don says, "from reading and school? Insects were so much bigger during the time of the dinosaurs because our atmosphere was different. The oxygen content used to be higher." His eyes move from dark object to dark object in the storm. "But then there are also all those old science fiction movies with massive bugs. Those were supposedly caused by radiation, though. You know, the *rawr rawr* bugs as big as Buicks thing."

Athena grumbles. "I don't think radiation works that way."

Images flash across her mind. Burns. Skin melting. Slow, painful death.

Don shrugs. "Something is making them bigger."

"You were *just* talking about the oxygen concentration thing."

"True. . .Maybe fifteen years without industry allowed the atmosphere to clean itself."

Athena sighs. She doesn't really care. The bugs—regardless of *why* they're larger—and the storms are two more obstacles in her way to California. She'll have to hope the Hellcat's shutters can withstand the wind. The debris. The bugs are gonna necessitate more ammo.

Don looks to Athena. "There is one thing the radiation caused for sure."

* * *

Athena mutters curses to herself as Don leads her up the stairs to the roof. Fuck does she wanna go outside in the storm for? On the top of a building? Feels like a shit idea.

Plus it's getting dark. Real dark. Gonna be a night so black there's no hope of a moon in all these nightmarish storm clouds.

How's she gonna be able to see anything? Even now?

At the door to the outside, Don hands her a hardhat. A pair of safety goggles. A respirator mask that fits over her nose and mouth.

She eyes them. Frowns. Then puts em on.

Don does the same. Unlocks the heavy bolt that keeps the metal entryway impassable. Then turns the handle.

The screeching wind catches the door. Pulls it out on its hinges. It slams against the side of the roof exit.

Athena instinctively flinches. Squints. She follows Don as he reaches for a guide rope. They walk to the edge of the building.

The sun continues its slow descent. Circle the size of a nickel trying to stay yellow but becoming orange and red. It sits on the horizon. A hazy, glowing sliver. Not much light gets through the storm.

Don points to the streets below. Then points to his ears. *Listen.*

Athena leans over. Stares down.

It's hard to make out definite details. But she sees black shapes. The bugs. They scuttle. Occasionally clash. From this height, they look almost normal-sized.

After a moment, more shapes join the fray. Human shapes. Or vaguely-human shapes. Figures that lope and jog. Run amongst their own numbers. Attack the bugs with something in their hands.

Maybe rocks. Shards of metal or concrete. No way to know.

Athena does *hear* em though. Even through the din of the storm. Screams. Shrieks. The human-shapes yell like crazed murderers. They only stop when they're outta breath. Then it starts all over again.

High-pitched insanity.

Impossible to tell which side is winning in the melee on the streets. There are plenty of bodies. As many humanoid as insectoid.

Which leads all the creatures to take momentary snack breaks.

Their unseen mouths and mandibles dig into the dead.

Cannibalism is rampant.

Athena watches for another few minutes.

Thinks: *Yeah, that's a good fuckin reason to stay off the streets.*

She taps Don on the shoulder. Jerks her head back toward the door. Follows the guide line back to the rooftop door.

Don hobbles behind. One hand cupped around his respirator mask to keep it from flying away. The other on the rope to keep *himself* from flying away. His damaged body ain't doing him any favors in this regard.

Athena at least got to walk away with a shiny new leg. Even if she hates it.

She helps Don get the door shut and barricaded again. Considers asking the brother why the *roof* is on lockdown. But realizes that when there's a gargantuan storm hurling giant goddamn bugs around like dandelion seeds, well, yeah: You keep the roof on lockdown.

Athena shakes the dust from her leathers. Hands back the helmet. Goggles. Respirator. She clears her throat. "Those were your muties?"

Don nods. "They hide or sleep in the sewers until it gets dark. Then they come out to forage." He pats himself down. "They aren't mutants, either. Some road runners passing through just called them that one day and it stuck. We think they're survivors— or were—who got badly burned by radiation and went mad. As if the radiation killed off the germ and the cancer. . . ."

Athena considers this. "Okay." Doesn't change the situation.

"Dan and I tried to talk to them once." He gestures around his face. "Their skin hangs in all these awful ways." His eyes drop. "All they do is scream. Just. . .scream. Their eyes are aware, but they can't or won't communicate like human beings."

Athena shrugs. "Well, you said they were insane."

Don shakes his head. "If I can be honest for a moment?" Ain't really a question. "That isn't the part that freaks me out."

Athena locks eyes with him. Raises her eyebrows. As in: *Yeah, sure, spit it out.*

Don says, "They scream because they're in pain. Constant, unending pain." His eyes water. "I can't even imagine how wretched of a life that must be."

She sniffs.

Wants to say: *These lunatic fuckballs have the benefit of being too outta their minds to care. You're stuck in your shit body with a mind intelligent enough to be* aware *of how screwed you are. That is wretched.*

Says instead: "I need to keep moving. I'm gonna need ammo. Maybe guns. Food. Water. Gas *and* whatever you know about stores of gas on my route west." Athena points her finger at Don. "I did your interview. I want what I'm owed."

Don frowns. "Y-yeah. That's fine. We can get you what you need." He scratches his chin. "But for the gas, you're going to have to talk to Crazy Mason. He's the gas man."

* * *

Athena sees Mark and Michelle both drying their hair in the lobby that now acts as a kind of visitors' lounge. She scowls at em. At once disliking their getting too cozy and feeling somewhat jealous that they can relax.

Mark sees the look. Smirks. Closes one eye at her. "If you don't take advantage of the fact that we can shower here—one of those pressure showers they sell for camping, but with hot water—then, woman, I feel sorry for you."

Athena rocks on her hips. Waits a beat. Holds up the key fob to the Hellcat. Tells Mark, "Move a week's worth of food and water to the car. I'll check storage later for ammo."

Mark silently shakes his head. "What if those things down there see me?"

Athena shrugs.

Dan holds up a hand. "No, now—"

Don talks behind Athena. Speaks as he moves behind her to the middle of the room. "We keep the elevator shut down at night. And during the storms. It's too risky."

Athena frowns. Looks to Mark again. Points. "Fine. Get our supplies ready. Keep it nearby so we can move." She snaps her fingers at Michelle. "You too, since it ain't much work till the morning."

Michelle groans. Comfy in a fat armchair. Leaning back. Can of warm Chef Boyardee in her fingers. She plunges her spoon into the ravioli. "When we're done eating."

She locks eyes with Athena.

Athena glowers. Mocks her. Says, "When we're done" in a snarky voice.

Michelle shrugs. "Yeah. When we're done." She swallows another spoonful of garbage food. "We're entitled to a break.

This's the first time our hosts haven't tried to kill, rape, or eat us." She licks her lips. "Plus, hey, my baby is due in. . .soon. Gimme a break."

Athena watches her. Watches this petulant pregnant chick. Then it turns into a useless staring contest. The young woman not giving anything up to the older road runner. And vice versa.

Michelle acts like she's won. Says to Dan, "Do you have any milk?"

Dan peels his eyes away from Athena. Nods. "Powdered milk, sure."

Athena turns to Don. Scowls at him. "Fuck's the shower in this place?"

"T-there's one in each bathroom. One in the women's and one in the men's." He bites his lip. "It just seemed to make sense to set it up that way."

"Do you actually get so many people through here that that's necessary?"

"Uh—" Don frowns. Looks to his brother.

Dan shrugs. Shakes his head.

Don says, "A few every month?" His voice unsure. "Road runners from the southern states. The east coast. We have a lot of fans." He flashes a faltering smile.

Athena cocks an eye. "Nobody from the west? California or Washington?"

Don chuckles. Catches himself. "I'm not sure if. . . I don't know how much more obvious this can all be. *Nothing* comes from the wastes except the storms and the bugs." He squints. "The west is just. . .death and dust."

Athena grunts. Sees Mark and Michelle staring at her. She doesn't blink. "I'm hitting the shower. Then we rest. When I wake up—"

she eyeballs Dan and Don without acknowledging what either has said "—we're talking to this Mason motherfucker. Then we're on the road." She lights a cigarette. "And we're heading west."

* * *

Athena locks the door to the women's bathroom. It's small. A tight, white-tiled room with a drain in the center. Toilet. Sink. The plastic shower head hangs from a hole in the ceiling panels. A Zodi camping contraption attached to a battery-powered water pump and a propane tank. With a feeder line plunged into the back of the toilet.

She strips. Places the bar of Irish Spring and the towel Don gave her on the edge of the sink. Bottle of whiskey too. She tucks her worn leathers in a corner with the hope that they won't get wet.

Sighs.

Mutters, "Where the hell was I that last time I had a warm shower?"

She stands under the shower head. Hits the button on the battery pump.

Water pours over her. It's hot. Amazing.

For a full minute, she doesn't move. Just waits. Wraps her arms around herself. Shifts her weight from one foot to the other. It's so fuckin nice she doesn't know what to do with herself other than enjoy it.

She reaches for the soap. Moves her hands down her sides.

That's when she feels it.

The skin on her right thigh.

The way it rises up along the seam where her flesh meets the chrome prosthesis. The part of her that's a machine now.

Athena stops. Stares at her feet. The left, calloused and mistreated. The right, shiny and metal. The wiggles the toes on her left. Then her right.

A sob escapes her lips. Then a pitiful moan.

Then Athena can't stop crying.

Hot water splashes against her shuddering back.

More than a decade of grief, loss, hate and anger comes pouring from her. Her fists clench and unclench. Her throat clicks when she tries to halt the sadness.

But she can't hold it in. Can't hold it back.

And so, she abuses the water supply. The heat.

Athena sits on the tiles. Tucks her human leg under the cool metal of her inhuman leg. She grabs the booze. Takes a massive pull. Coughs. Leans outta the range of the water and lights a damp cigarette from the pack in her jacket.

She stays like that for twenty minutes.

Grieves. Allows herself to be weak.

Not that she'll ever let the others see this part of her.

6.

The morning is dim. Dirty. Dusty.

Athena stumbles from her cot in one of the empty offices. Knocks over a half-gone bottle of whiskey. Curses. Rights it. Then ambles toward the smell of coffee and toast. Lights a cigarette while she walks. More or less in a straight line.

She finds the others back in the food room. She figured she'd be the first up to face the day but. . .it wasn't exactly a good night.

So fuck it.

Don offers her a little wave. Gestures toward her with a hot cup of coffee in his other hand.

Dan sits with Mark and Michelle. Regaling the both of em with more stories about radio and music. The brother and sister nod respectfully.

Michelle smiles more.

And Athena's pretty damn sure she can see Dan blush.

Which is sweet.

And also precisely the opposite fuckin mood Athena's in right now.

She takes her coffee from Dan. Breathes smoke. Looks to Mark and Michelle. "You gather up the supplies?"

Mark jerks his head in the direction of the visitors area. "Yeah. The Brothers-D here loaded us up." He digs into his shirt pocket. Produces two bottles of Advil. "Even got some medical supplies." He winks. "Y'know. For those bad hangovers."

Dan cranes his neck to face Athena. "We're happy to help."

Athena watches him for a minute. Gives an almost-imperceptible nod. Walks off to see what's gotta be loaded into the Hellcat.

There's two pallets of canned food—twenty-four cans in each. One is Chef Boyardee spaghetti and meatballs. The other is Campbell's chicken noodle. Next to that is about five gallons of drinking water. Two boxes of powdered milk. Fake eggs. Fake butter. Sugar. Diapers. Baby formula. Motor oil. Radiator fluid. Cartons of cigarettes. Ammo for the Springfield Armory 1911 *and* the sawed-off shotgun. As well as a couple spare pump 12-gauges.

Athena sips her coffee. Smokes her smoke.

Thinks: *Shit.*

These two brothers *are* goddamn angels. Saints.

She gathers up some of the supplies. Heads to the elevator.

* * *

Other than the half-inch of dust that covers everything, you'd never guess at the chaos that occurred on Columbus's streets the night before. There're no signs of the muties or the bugs. No bodies. No blood. The wind'll carry away even the dust after a while. Everything will return to its abandoned look.

Till the next storm, anyway.

The Hellcat, on the other hand, could use a wash. It's caked in crap.

Athena makes a *tsk* noise. Finds the key fob in her coat pocket. Pops the trunk. Which sends a light cloud of dust up into the air.

She stashes the supplies. Walks around her baby. Gingerly wiping dirt and grime from the windows.

In the end, her clothing ends up being dustier than the car.

Athena decides that this is how things should be.

She starts the car. Returns to the trunk.

* * *

Athena doesn't say anything. Just puts the fresh cookies on the table in the food room. A dozen. More than she's made for any one group.

Dan and Don gawk at the treats. Then at Athena.

She's a golden goddess. A hero to be revered.

The brothers reach for the cookies. Taste em. Savor em.

They allow themselves to have only one each.

Dan licks his lips. "We're going to save the rest in the fridge. This is amazing. Thank you."

Athena offers em another barely-perceptible nod. Says, "Where's Crazy Mason."

Don dabs his index finger against the table. Uses it to pick up errant crumbs that then end up in his mouth. "Mason stays at the BP station on Neil Avenue. It's just northwest of here. You'll see the smoke. That's Mason refining crude."

Dan picks up the loose cookies. Puts em on a paper plate he plucks from nearby. "He's fortified the whole thing with walls and barbed wire. Plus, the streets nearby are booby-trapped. We radioed him to tell him you were going to stop by, but my advice is to stop your car a block or two away and walk so he can see you."

"Yeah, and, uh. . .none of you are Muslim, right?"

"Yeah, and, uh. . .don't talk about his wife."

* * *

Dan and Don help move the rest of the supplies into the Hellcat's trunk.

Once again, Athena's fully stocked.

Even has a few special bottles of whiskey from the D's.

It's comforting. One thing in her life that's less-fucked.

Mark shakes hands with the two brothers. Smiles.

Michelle hugs em. Gives each a gentle kiss on the cheek. Says, "We'll be listening for you guys for as long as we can."

Dan and Don blush. Shuffle their feet. Like, *Aww shucks.*

For Athena, they merely grin. Nod their heads.

She nods back. Gives em a thumbs-up. Slides into the driver's seat. Guns the engine. Guides the Hellcat back down into Columbus. Makes a right on North High Street. A left on West Goodale Street.

There's a huge park to their right. The once thriving vein of the 670 highway to their left.

The houses and buildings here bleed into more suburbia. A strange mash of family homes with yards and an apartment complex.

Athena turns right onto Neil Avenue. Slows the car when she can see the obvious fortifications down the way. Ten-foot walls.

Wood reinforced with scrap metal. Barbed wire *everywhere*. And the smoke, of course. That fat black cloud of smoke.

She stops. Opens her door. Steps out.

Mark and Michelle follow suit.

Athena looks over her shoulder. Says to the two, "Stay behind me."

Might sound like concern for their wellbeing, but mostly, Athena doesn't want either of em to set off any booby-traps. Fuck up the works here.

She walks along the blacktop. Between the grass- and tree-lined sidewalks. Her eyes are wide. Alert. The hangover in her brain and stomach fades. She focuses on the husks of cars. Looks for tripwires. Pits designed to trap mutants or bugs.

So far, nothing.

Doesn't mean the traps ain't there.

Or maybe Crazy Mason moved em.

Shit. Who knows.

She sees the dude standing up on the wall closest to Neil Avenue. Crazy Mason. A skinny, bearded, aging sonuvabitch in camouflage hunting clothes. Hair back in a ponytail. Repeating rifle in his hands. Aimed at the three walking down the street toward him.

Some fuckin Ted Nugent-type marching the perimeter of his fort along the walls.

Athena mutters, "Christ." Low, under her breath.

Crazy Mason shouts: "Y'all them fuckers the radio retards told me about?"

Mark mutters, "Christ." Low, under his breath.

Athena puts her hands up. Hisses in a whisper to Mark: "Yeah. My gut feeling is to make sure this guy doesn't know you like dick."

"You're a charmer. Liking dick is not a precursor to liking *dicks*, is the thing. And this guy sounds like a real dick."

Athena shouts back to Crazy Mason. "I'm—" She stops. Furrows her brow. "I'm the Hellcat. These two are with me. I need gas. And I need to know where to get gas on my way west."

Mason laughs. "West? Jesus, little lady. What the hell you want out west?"

Athena sniffs. *Little lady.* . . . Says, "That's my business."

Mason rests his rifle on his shoulder. "That so? Then, I'm not really sure why your business needs to have anything to do with mine." He spits. Chuckles. Grumbles.

Then he leans over. Acts like he's listening to someone inside the compound. Shouts back to this unseen person: "Well, Jesus, if she's gonna be such a bitch about it, I dunno why I need to help her *at all.*" More listening. "Nah, I helped them retard freaks on account of they play the music I like. I don't know this woman at all." More listening. "All right. . . *All right,* Carol."

He turns back to Athena. "My wife says I should help you. It's the Christian thing to do. And she's right." Spit. "You're gonna wanna turn left. Use the sidewalk there. Do *not* step on the slabs with little red X's on em. Then head for the front gate, but do *not* step on any raised patches. They's all boom-booms."

* * *

Athena weaves her way through whatever IEDs Mason has set up. Tries to make sure Mark and Michelle don't step on one and cut the day short.

The three wait in front of Mason's gate. Somewhat sloppy two-by-fours nailed and screwed together with scrap metal interlaced.

Ain't pretty, but it works. Since this motherfucker and his wife have survived the madness of Columbus's mutie-bug nights for. . . . Well, however long they've been here.

Athena knocks.

Mason calls out from inside. "Don't get yer panties in a bunch."

Athena rolls her head back. Cracks her neck.

Be easier to kill this cocksucker and loot his shit. As usual. But that might leave Dan and Don vulnerable. Since they rely on this guy for gas and electrical work.

So Athena takes a breath. Waits. Listens as an engine chugs to life behind the walls.

Then the front wall itself moves. It slides to the right.

Mason's entire front gate is a massive wall built into a Mack truck.

Athena nods in appreciation.

It's a good idea.

Take a couple of bulldozers to knock it back.

Inside, it's gas pumps. A greenhouse. Farther back is a vehicle repair station. And an office that's clearly Mason's bedroom. There's a mattress inside. Plus an amazing number of empty beer bottles. No sign of the wifey yet.

Mason reverses the truck once the trio are inside. He hops outta the cab. Rifle still in his hands. He eyeballs Mark and Michelle and Athena. Her guns. He spits. "Ma'am, goes without sayin, but if your hands get too close to those guns, I'll drop you." Alcohol on his breath.

Athena crosses her arms over her chest. "Just need gas. Information."

"Uh huh." Mason nods. "The 'how much' is what I need to know. Seein as how I gotta brew up all the go-juice myself here."

His eyes flit toward the pillar of smoke. The grungy steel exhaust port it spews from.

Athena sniffs. "Right."

Mark says, "You're actually *refining* here? How?"

Mason plays with the tobacco in his cheek. Narrows his eyes at Mark. "Thanks." He spits. "You sound. . .educated. You went to school and all that. One'a them faggy East Coast Ivy League fuckers." He points at Mark's face. "But you don't know a damn thing about turning crude into go-juice, do you?"

Mark furrows his brow. Seems standoffish for a second. Then shakes his head. "No."

Athena watches Mason's hands. Watches the way he holds his rifle. Just in case this guy wants to move fast and put a bullet in one of her big commodities. She uncrosses her arms. Lets her hands dangle at her sides. Near the 1911. Near the shotgun.

Mason says, "You run the crude through a high-pressure steam boiler. Crude turns into different shit at different temperatures. So you turn it inta vapor and collect the vapor. You follow, college boy?"

Mark nods.

Mason says, "Shit's called a distillation column. Okay? So you boil the crude. Feed the vapors into a distillation column." Mason walks toward Mark. His voice gets louder. But the gun stays low. "The vapors travel up. Cool. Condense. Different trays collect the liquids at different heights." Mason spits. Licks his lips. Shouts. "And *that* is why *my* redneck ass actually *means* something now that the world is over." He juts his chin at Athena. Michelle. "I *matter*. My wife is finally happy. What do you people do, anyway? Other than *take*?"

Mark sucks in his cheeks. Frowns and arches his eyebrows. Nods. "I'm a doctor. I, uh—" He shrugs. "I try to save people."

Michelle holds her belly. "I'd like to prevent the human race from going extinct."

Athena keeps her mouth shut.

Mason blinks. Like his brain is slowly registering all this. He wheels on Mark. "You're a doctor?"

Mark clears his throat. "That's what I went to those *faggy* schools for."

Mason nods. "Yeah. Yeah, okay." He snaps his fingers. "Then you gotta help my wife out before I give you the gas."

Athena has zero reaction to any of this. Her preference remains: Shoot this strange fucker and get gone.

Her fingers twitch at her sides.

Her guns feel so close by.

"Of course." Mark smiles. "What's bothering her?"

"Bad, bad pain in her side." Mason looks toward his ramshackle bedroom. All the empty bottles there. The crummy mattress. "We're thinkin it might be her appendix or something. Y'know, if it's gone rotten."

Mark scratches his cheek. "Okay." He looks to Athena and Michelle. Back to Mason. "Shouldn't take me more than a couple minutes to figure out. Uh. . . ." He shrugs. "Why don't you show me to your wife." Another smile.

Mason waves the group on.

They follow him into the service station. The door on it still listing the hours of business. Little plastic sign saying WELCOME! COME IN!

Mason says, "Hey, babe."

The group tracks his eyes to a skeletal corpse in the corner. Skin papery. Cracked. Yellow. This corpse silent. Motionless on a rocking chair behind the register.

Mark sighs.

Athena ain't shocked at all. Seems par for the course to her.

Mason gingerly steps over to the rotting body. Runs his fingers through its straw-like hair. He kisses her forehead. "Carol, honey, I did what you said. We're gonna give these folks some gas. And the faggot's gonna check and make sure you're okay."

Mark rubs his forehead.

Athena fights the urge to light a cigarette. No telling what kinda explosive fumes are floating around this place. Best not to, but, man, what a mercy killing.

Mason gestures to the carcass of Carol. Says to Mark, "Okay, doc. See what you can tell us." He points again. Laughs. "But don't get any funny ideas touching my woman."

Mark plays along. Throws his hands up. "No, of course not." He walks around the counter. "I'm just a faggot, right?" He kneels before the dead woman. Probes her sides with his fingers. Acts cool. Professional. In spite of the utter ridiculousness. "Ah. All right. So. . . ."

He wipes his brow. Makes a little show of it. Makes like he's deep in thought. Feels the corpse's sides again. "There *is* some inflammation. The, uh, pain she's feeling? The bloating? I think it's a gas buildup. It's not appendicitis." He smiles. "We shouldn't have to operate."

Mason nods. "Wow, doc. Okay. That's a big load off."

"Bet it is. I'm a little worried, though. What's her food intake like?"

Mason looks around at nothing. "I mean. . . ." Shrugs. "Same crap as always. Stuff I can get from hunting. Bugs. Mutie meat." He clicks his tongue. "Always cook it real thorough like though. Pop."

"Pop?"

"Yeah, man. Soda pop. She likes pop."

"Okay." Mark nods. Pats Carol's knee. "Okay, I think for a while, you're gonna need to cut pop out of the equation. Drink more water. The carbonation, the fizzy stuff in pop, that's going to make Carol feel more bloated. It just adds gas." He stands. Twists the cap on one of the Advil bottles. Doles out about ten little brown pills. Turns to Mason. Pills in his palm. "Make sure Carol takes one of these in the morning and then one at night. With water. She should be feeling good in no time."

The smiles again.

Fake as shit but convincing.

Mason's fuckin thrilled, though. He laughs. Grabs the Advil. Pockets it. Punches Mark's shoulder. Rubs the shoulders of his deceased wife. Looks to the group. "God, doc. That's great. That's goddamn great." He laughs again. "I knew the Lord would provide." He claps. Clicks his tongue. "Even now, you showing up here. The Lord does watch."

Smile.

Athena's still silent.

Mason beams. Grins. "It's a trinity. Father. Son. Holy Spirit. Always works in threes. Yup." Mason clasps the shoulder of Carol's corpse. "So if it's threes, then let's say thirty gallons of real go-juice."

Holy shit.

Now Athena talks. "That sounds right."

Mason tucks his rifle into a corner. Apparently not thinking he needs it to scare the shit outta anyone right now. He points to Athena. "Y'all are goin west, yeah?"

Athena fidgets. Sniffs. She doesn't wanna tell anyone anything. And also wants a fuckin smoke. Says, "California."

"Hoo. Little lady, thirty gallons won't get you to California. Especially not with that big V8. It's all I can spare right now, but it won't do you much."

Athena looks from Mason to Carol's eyeless body. Then out the station windows. "It'll get us outta here." She grunts. "What I wanna have is a map of the west. Areas we can resupply. Get fuel."

Mason bites his lip. Pats Carol's shoulder. "Yeah. I know." A pause. "You sure?" A pause. "All right." He meets Athena's eyes. "There's one thing that runs in the west. One thing."

He makes the sign of the cross.

"I never told'em retard brothers about it cuz I don't want em telling anyone. Broadcasting all this. . . . Those two live in their own world. The insulation. Makes em two and others feel all right. Kinda like nothin is wrong." Mason's lips become a tight line. "West *is* death and dust for folks from the east. California, I don't know nothin about. Whatever you're looking for there. But the Trackers might."

Athena rolls her tongue around in her cheeks. "Trackers?"

"Where I get my crude from. Trackers. They run the rails. All the old Amtrak lines. They go as far south as Texas for the crude, then they go east to Atlanta. After that, the road runners pick up solid work moving it along the coast." He shrugs. "Hell, I usually take my F250 and trailer to Indianapolis and get barrels there in exchange for the brothers doing what they do—since they can't put out music without constant electricity. Was there to restock, just before the storm. Got here as the dust started to hit. Anyway, they oughtta still be there. Takes em about five days on either side of the trip to repair and get themselves back together. All that."

"Trains." Athena shakes her head. Confusion and recognition. "You're talking about *trains*."

Mason nods. "Trains." He lets go of his dead wife for a moment. "Ain't got all the lines running. It's pretty limited. But if you wanna get to California, you're gonna have to talk to the Trackers."

"How far are they?"

"Already said. Indianapolis. That's the real start of the wastes, where everything is grey and dead." Mason looks to Carol's body. Looks to Michelle. Mark. Athena. "I'll pray for you. Cuz like I said, Easterners don't last much out there."

7.

Athena spends a few minutes looking over Mason's maps. It's a straight shot on I-70. Nothing complicated there. Shouldn't take more'n two and a half hours. Less if she guns it.

What concerns her are the spots circled in red. *WRAITHS: DON'T STOP* written next to one outside Dayton. Another outside Richmond.

She's heard the term before. Wraiths. Doesn't have a clue what they are. Which holds for every damn boogeyman drunkards talk about in bars. Not exactly reliable. Just names. Terms.

Athena picks up the two fifteen-gallon gas cans for the Hellcat. Feels the muscles in her arms strain. Thinks: *Sure woulda been nice if I coulda parked the car closer.*

* * *

Athena lets Mark and Michelle do the goodbyes themselves. Mason was useful, but they're losing time. She wants to get to

Indianapolis as soon as possible. And she's still pretty goddamn cranky.

This whole endeavor was supposed to be a solo trip west.

Ain't working out that way.

She'd thought it'd be easy to trek alone. Thought that if ninety-percent of the world's population keeled over, she wouldn't run into so many motherfuckers.

But, man, even these walking dead have a nasty habit of clinging to some kinda life.

Boring. Broadly insane. Life.

Athena tiptoes around Mason's booby-traps. Steers clear of anything with a red mark on it. Really doesn't wanna explode at this point in her journey.

She tucks the gas into the trunk. The fuel nestled between diapers and ammunition. Athena lights a cigarette.

Looks west.

The wind kicks up. Pushes its way through the trees. The leaves. Acts like it wants to tug at her leather jacket. Leather pants. But doesn't have the strength.

* * *

The Hellcat offers the world a full-throated roar. The engine eats gas as though it was starved.

Michelle leans forward in the passenger seat. Turns on the radio. The voices of both Dapper Dan and Dapper Don float into the air. The bastards sound identical so there's no way to know whose voice is whose.

"—just watched the *legendary* Hellcat boogie outta the city limits."

"Yup. Yup. She was. . .uh. . . ."

"She was a bit of a handful."

"'No nonsense' is how I'd describe her. That is a little more respectful."

"That's only because you have a crush on her."

"Oh, jeez, okay. Give me a break there."

"Fine." Laugh. Laugh track. "Fine, I relent. Though, as your older brother, I feel it is part of my familial *obligation* to make you a little crazy."

"Oh, is that right? You're older by, what, twenty or thirty seconds?" Laugh.

"I still think it counts!" More laughing. From the both of em. "Anyway, this one goes out to the Hellcat and her companions. Creedence Clearwater Revival with 'Run Through the Jungle.' Safe travels, guys. We'll be playing for *you* until you can't hear us anymore!"

CCR fades up.

Athena ain't thrilled to be attached to the song. Ain't thrilled at being called "a handful" either. But it's a good tune. And, she supposes, it does fit.

She grips the wheel. Keeps em moving across the blacktop.

I-70 has been picked clean by scavengers, like the vast majority of other asphalt veins. Few, if any, wrecks remain.

So Athena lays on the speed. Let's the car climb to eighty. Ninety. A hundred. It feels right to leave Columbus in the rearview. Even if Mark and Michelle might've thought they could get by there for a while. The ignorance of the brothers who're supposed to be disseminating information doesn't really bolster that idea.

There's a subtle shift in the shades of the plants around em. Columbus was a dead town, but the vegetation was doing its best to take over. The flora grew fat and green and lush on carcasses. Just like the east coast. Where lawns were forests.

Here. . . .

Here, the plants turn pale. Lighter variations on the green theme.

Be easy enough for someone to think it's the change in seasons. If you weren't paying attention to the other nagging details. The increase in dirt. The dead grass.

Long tracts of what was formerly farmland that swirls now with dust devils. Mini-tornadoes of dried out dirt and rocks.

Everything is just. . .dehydrated. Desaturated.

All this maddeningly flat, empty space.

Athena sniffs. Lights a cigarette.

Pushes the pedal till the Hellcat's cranking along at one-twenty.

Not the fastest she's ever driven. But the highest speed she's ever inflicted on any passengers.

Her eyes flit right. Over to Michelle's face. The pregnant woman's lips pulled into a tight, bloodless line.

Then up into the rearview mirror. To see Mark's eyes. The brother's pupils big and black like manhole covers.

Athena breathes smoke. Smiles a little.

Scaring the brother and sister ain't quite the goal.

Getting a bit of a reaction from toying with em gives her a bit of a grin though.

Mark and Michelle's smiles become concern.

Athena's concern becomes a quiet thrill.

And the world fades to grey.

Inch by inch.

Mile by mile.

All along the asphalt veins.

Athena keeps her hands steady on the wheel. Moves her ass around in the driver's seat to keep it from falling asleep.

They close in on Dayton.

She hears the steady whir of the gears. Lets the engine find a nice rhythm at about eighty.

Athena moves her hands. Keeps the right at the apex of the steering wheel. Just cruising. She holds the sawed-off with her left. Pulls it from its holster. Rides with it in her lap as she passes through those areas marked in red by Mason.

Nothing happens.

So much for Mason's warning about Wraiths.

She sure as shit doesn't stop.

But all the same, nothing happens.

The Hellcat blows by Dayton. "Run Through the Jungle" long since replaced by some classic rock and now AC/DC's "Highway to Hell." Athena wonders, again, if the brothers' song choices ain't a bit too on the nose.

They close in on Indianapolis. The acres of land on both sides of the highway continue to show their decay. Green and yellow becoming grey to match the pavement.

The number of dust devils increases too. No longer one or two sparse little twisters. Now there are dozens that spin in and out of existence. A dance party of whipping winds.

Amid all of it is the dominant insect life. A congregation of grasshoppers with black stripes on their fat back legs gathers in a field. More than a dozen. The size of golden retrievers. Their antennae bounce back and forth. They turn their bodies to observe the roaring Hellcat.

Mark taps the window in the back. "Anyone else see that?" *Tap tap taptaptap.* "Holy shit."

Athena pumps the brakes. Brings the car down to thirty. Twenty. Full-stop. She cranes her neck so she can see what's got the doctor so excited.

Hard to tell at first, but she sees the shape. It's a hundred feet behind the grasshoppers. Spindly red translucent front legs arched in the grass. The rear legs pale. Almost light. Those legs are all attached to a dark red, shiny thorax. It ain't moving. It's waiting. The grasshoppers don't see it.

They're distracted.

That's when the running spider launches its ambush. It hauls ass. Legs a blur. It tackles the nearest grasshopper. The others flee in a rush. Leap thirty feet forward. Right toward the Hellcat. Leap again. An insect stampede. They land with heavy thuds around the Dodge. Their powerful legs piston against the asphalt. Membranous wings push the air. Create enough wind to rock the Hellcat on its suspension. They jump and jump and jump.

Athena blinks. Thinks: *Well, fuck.* Looks back at the titanic tussle between the grasshopper and the spider.

It's a mad thrash of legs and dust being thrust into the air. Green grey kicking out. Red curling in. The spider drives its venomous fangs into the grasshopper over and over. Pins the bug. Holds it while the biological poisons do their work.

Other than the sounds of violence, the creatures are silent. There's no roaring or screaming. Nothing. Only the occasional wet *crunch.*

After a moment, the grasshopper loses its will to fight. It slows. Its antennae flick less. It struggles less. And then the whole thing over.

The dog-sized spider carries the dog-sized grasshopper in its mandibles.

Athena watches Michelle's hands mindlessly caress her belly.

Mark's face is contorted in disgust. He cocks his head to the side. Listening for something.

Athena hears it too. Some kind of buzz. Same as a bee or a—

"Holy *shit*," Mark says. His eyes dart up. "Wasp."

A wasp. Vicious-looking. All black with bright red-orange legs. It flies in loops. Wings buzz so fast and loud that they drown out everything but the thrum of the Hellcat's Hemi engine.

The mean bastard loop-de-loops. Hovers near the Hellcat's windshield. Coloring of the car similar to its own. The red and black. Its legs hang. Not limp. Twitching. The stinger in its ass emerges just a little. Toxins from the tip ooze.

Like this fucker's trying to figure out if it should sting the Hellcat.

Athena doubts it could get through the metal, but it's the biggest bug they've seen. About the size of a great dane. So she keeps the shotgun ready.

Then, in a blink, the wasp takes off toward the spider.

The spider realizes it's in trouble. Senses it somehow. Runs, but doesn't drop its prize.

The wasp plows into the spider's midsection. Stings and stings. Quick as a whip. Then it backs off. Waits. Hovers. Takes its time as the spider succumbs to a similar paralyzing agent as it inflicted on the grasshopper.

Athena cocks an eye. Wonders if the grasshopper could ever understand the concept of *schadenfreude*. Or if the spider would "get" the irony of this madness.

The wasp plucks up the spider. Shoots into the air. Then off.

Then it's quiet again.

Athena grunts. Hits the gas. Gets em back up to eighty.

Mark slouches in the backseat. "Spider wasps are terrifying. They paralyze the spider and take it back to their nest. Then lay an egg on it." He readjusts his butt to get more comfortable. Looks out the window. Maybe for more monstrous insects. "Then the larva hatches and it devours the internal organs of the paralyzed spider."

Athena grips the steering wheel. "We ain't going outside for a while."

8.

They follow I-70 south. Indianapolis looms off to the right.

As far as buildings go, this city has more big ones than Columbus. Some brick. Older structures. But also glass and steel skyscrapers. Family homes there around the edges near the highway.

This is the only difference Athena notices.

It's all still flat, indistinct land to her. Might as well be a boring foreign country.

The other thing it seems to share with Columbus is the lack of a population.

Makes Athena think about the screaming muties and the scuttling bugs. Weird little things hidden under the surface.

She also has no real idea where she's going. Mason said to meet the Trackers at the Amtrak station on. . .South Illinois Street. Wherever the fuck that is. Supposed to be near the stadium.

Athena didn't wanna putter around inside the city itself, so she's still on the highway. Follows it south. The road bends west.

But now she's bored and doesn't wanna aimlessly circle the whole damn town.

So she glides the Hellcat into the rightmost lane toward exit 79B. Which at least seems to head back into the heart of the city.

The off ramp puts em on Madison Avenue. After the first intersection, Athena slows and reads the beat-up blue sign that greets em:

Welcome to
Downtown
Indianapolis
Crossroads of America

Athena sniffs. Kills the radio so she can concentrate. Looks around.

Sure as shit doesn't seem like "downtown" anything.

Trees with grey leaves line the four-lane avenue. There are a few buildings behind em. Maybe apartments or offices. Some parking lots.

That's about it.

Farther down are more squat buildings. Brick and concrete. One short fat one's a Clear Channel HQ. The tall place next to it is utterly vacant.

Another ghost town.

One with shitloads of parking.

The trees give way to more empty streets.

They cross South Street. Off to the left is the big barn-shaped stadium. Brick and dark glass with metal scaffolding on top.

The train station is just ahead. A big sucker with a brick base and metal siding above. Can't pull into the closest lot, though. Whole thing's been barricaded with concrete blocks and sandbags.

So Athena drives a little farther, where Madison becomes Meridian for no good reason. She heads under a long white overpass that proclaims they're in the "Wholesale District." The thing's a tunnel. Dark. No sun. No lights. Just steel beams and their rusty rivets.

There are more barriers—or something—at the other end of the tunnel.

She thinks the whole time that they're being herded. Safe bet on a tough gamble. Not a lot to be done about it.

Whatever gets her to the redwoods.

On the other hand: Fuck this.

She throws the Hellcat into reverse. Floors it.

Michelle digs her palms into the dash to keep from slamming into it.

Mark is chucked forward. His nose smashes sideways against Michelle's seat.

Athena spins the wheel. Backs onto South Street. Heads west. Keeps the train station to their right.

They pass another barricaded parking lot. This one with a hint of life: Someone's silhouette far back against a brick wall.

She makes a right on Illinois Street. A big Greyhound Bus terminal sits to the left. Snuggled up against the Amtrak station.

And there's another tunnel. More darkness. More steel beams.

Athena rubs her face.

The Hellcat idles.

No good options here.

She lights another cigarette. Hands the sawed-off to Michelle. Pulls her stainless steel Springfield Armory 1911. Grunts. Rolls the Hellcat forward.

They creep through the tunnel. Dust clouds in faint wisps in the Hellcat's running lights. Athena stops the car at the next barricade. The concrete and sandbags.

Athena turns the engine off. Holds tight.

In the silence she hears the deep hum of a diesel engine nearby.

The train.

Or trains.

Who goddamn knows.

Athena waits a little more. Listens. Smokes and thinks. Squints. Frowns.

Then opens her door and steps into the darkness. She holsters her 1911. Doesn't put her hands up but keeps em loose. Nonthreatening.

She approaches the barrier. Face blank. Eyes flitting between possible ambush places. She flicks ash from her cigarette. Stands next to the barrier. It's just inside the tunnel.

Athena leans over. Looks to her left. Her right.

She snorts.

There are two teenagers on each side. Four in total. Fourteen. Fifteen. Sixteen. Seventeen. Boys and girls. Different ages. Different races. All of em dressed in khaki jumpsuits. All of em armed with what seem to be machine guns that're nicely tricked out. M4s and AKs or knockoffs sporting holoscopes at least.

One kid has an underslung grenade launcher.

All that firepower's pointed more or less in the direction of Athena's head. But they ain't shot her yet, so. . . .

Far as the kids go, they ain't too dirty or beat up. Look clean. Well fed.

Athena eyeballs the two on the left.

The two on the right.

After a minute of silence, says, "Your parents around?"

* * *

One of the teens gets into a nearby dirt-mover. Big sonuvabitch backhoe. The girl in the driver's seat uses the big metal bucket on the front of the backhoe to pull two concrete blocks away.

Athena half-heartedly offers the group a thumbs-up while the others point their guns at her and her Hellcat.

She pulls up. Into a sorta town square that's locked down by my concrete and sand. The side of one stumpy brick building says "Pan Am Plaza." Basically a one block-by-one block area with enough interlocking structures—plus the train station—to make its defensive appeal obvious. Seems as though it could withstand a siege.

The girl in the backhoe replaces the concrete barriers.

Now Athena's trapped.

With teenagers.

These young goofballs are the Trackers?

She and Mark and Michelle stay in the car. Athena smokes out the window but doesn't explain herself.

And fuck these kids anyway. They ain't so talkative themselves.

Just pointing guns around.

One—a white kid overburdened by freckles and a mop of brown hair—stares at Athena while she smokes. He stares and keeps his rifle aimed at her face.

She doesn't do anything but maintain eye contact.

Lets him know that if he wants to play predator, she bigger.

Badder.

Smoke and stare.

The 1911 always at the ready.

Then this sorta pudgy doofus arrives.

The kids all shout "Father Bill" like soldiers announcing the arrival of a commanding officer. They lower their weapons. Don't sling em, but lower em.

Father Bill. A clean-cut, brown-haired, middle-aged white guy with a bit of a gut. Early fifties. He wears the same khaki jumpsuit as the others. What differentiates his dress is the brown leather jacket. No rifle but a revolver on his hip.

Makes her think of General MacArthur. The World War II uber-commander. Which certainly ain't an accident.

Dude probably thinks of himself that way, too.

He's flanked by two women.

One, middle-aged. Maybe late forties. Slender with a round, slightly sunburned face. Rosy cheeks. Red hair tied back in a ponytail. Khakis. Lever-action rifle in her hands.

The second, probably their daughter. Around fifteen. Got the same kinda look as the other two. Narrower face than mom. Not sunburned, either, but tan. The same red hair in another ponytail. Khakis. Bolt-action rifle.

She stares at Athena.

They walk in tandem. Make their way toward the car from farther inside the open-air plaza.

Father Bill holds his hand up. Not quite a wave. Just an acknowledgement. "Good afternoon. I'm gonna guess that you're the three the Dapper brothers have been jawing about on the radio." He smirks. "The Hellcat and her crew. It's a gorgeous vehicle."

Athena steps outta the Dodge. Nods.

Mark and Michelle—radio in hand—do the same. Though they try to look friendlier than Athena with pleasant faces and genuine smiles.

Athena says, "You're the Trackers?"

Father Bill cocks his head. "Well, we're part of the Tracker family, sure."

The middle-aged woman elbows Father Bill. "I hate this false modesty crap." She frowns at her. . .husband? Mate? Doesn't sound like she's playing. "Without Bill, the Trackers wouldn't be able to function." She moves her eyes to meet Athena's. "*He* is the one who got all these big diesel engines working again, and it's about time those assholes in Houston showed him some respect."

Athena bites her lip. Takes a pull from her cigarette. "I. . . ." She shakes her head. "I don't care." Puts her hands on her hips. Thinks: *Whoopdee shit.*

The woman stops. Shuts her mouth. Blinks. "You're kind of a bitch, aren't you."

"Yeah. Whatever. We need to get to California. Mason? In Columbus? You donate barrels to him every month to keep the radio station going. He said you're the best chance we've got."

The redhead looks to Father Bill. "Your call."

Father Bill scratches his cheek. Considers it. "In spite of our religious nature—"

"We're a *Catholic* organization." The older redhead cocks an eye at Athena.

Like that should mean a damn thing to the Hellcat, but it doesn't.

Father Bill continues, "We don't offer free rides. I need to know how you can help us before I consider sending you west on one of our trains." He crosses his arms. "These are dark days for humanity and we don't know you at all. Allowing you access to our cargo would be. . .foolish." Offers a weak smile.

Athena shifts her weight from one foot to the other. Closes an eye. "I'm good with a gun. Can fix anything automotive. Bake, too." She jerks her head toward Michelle. "The pregnant chick's decent with a shotgun." She points over her shoulder to Mark. "He's a doctor."

Father Bill's face is expressionless.

The middle-aged woman's lips a thin line verging on a sneer. Obviously considers Athena to be a threat or an unholy hellion. Which ain't too far off.

The daughter, though. . . There's something else there. A twitch of the eyebrows. Recognition or hope. She never moves her eyes away from Athena.

The older woman sees it.

"Okay." Father Bill nods. "We need fighters. Badly. The Wraiths hit us hard on the way up from Texas. But there's no way I'm gonna put a pregnant woman's life—or her baby's—at risk." He smiles at Michelle. "There's precious little life left in this world as it is. You can surely help in the kitchen car, though."

Michelle chirps. "I'm happy to help."

Mark chimes in with her. "Same here. We've. . .seen horrible things recently. It would be nice to help the good guys instead of suffering for the whims of evil."

Athena grimaces at him. This waxing poetic garbage.

"Good," Father Bill says. "Good. I do have a few young Trackers in need of medical assistance. I'm hoping that a hand more skilled than mine can save them. . . ." His voice trails off.

Athena squints. Grinds her cigarette out on the pavement.

"You, Hellcat." Father Bill juts his head toward Athena. "If you have cargo in your vehicle that you need to bring, I can have some of my Trackers assist you in getting it stowed onboard the Tracker Bulldozer."

Athena grunts. "*Padre*, the car comes with me."

Father Bill arches his eyebrows. "Making room for your car means losing room for you and for freight—and we're supposed to deliver a thousand barrels of crude to Denver in exchange for livestock and dry goods."

"I can sleep in the Dodge."

"What about the extra cost to me in weight?"

Athena shrugs. "I'll just kill extra sonsabitches for you." She eyeballs the freckled kid who'd been pointing his gun at her head. "Like that little puke. I'll kill the shit outta him if he doesn't back off."

9.

They stand on the open-air platform of the elevated tracks at the Indianapolis Amtrak station. Athena. Mark. Michelle. Father Bill. The two women whose names remain unsaid.

The Tracker Bulldozer hisses in front of em. Eight big silver double-decker cars that sandwich four massive freight cars. Four on each side. Hydraulics and brakes expel steam and gases ahead of the next big haul.

It's an ugly behemoth. The Tracker Bulldozer has been cobbled together in a purely patchwork fashion. Scrap metal where some doors used to be. Barbed wire welded to windows that're cracked and will never open again. Rusty defensive spikes along the sides. The formerly-blue interiors now coated in grime and random strips of fabric to replace seats that've been ruined.

Whatever works.

And it does, apparently, work.

Except it's actually the "TrakER Bulldozer."

Someone took the liberty of erasing all the A's and M's from the Amtrak logos. Added a blue-stencil "ER" to the end.

Trakers and their Traker Bulldozer.

All of which causes Athena to reflexively pronounce it "Trayker" in her head.

She sniffs. Watches another dozen or so teens and folks in their twenties move supplies onto the train. Pallets of food and crates of ammo and fat metal barrels of crude are packed in using forklifts. A few grunts closer to Athena's age supervise. She guesses there are thirty or forty people at work in total here.

And, hey, good for the Trakers. Must be nice to have an organized militia to protect your interests. Except why are more'n half of em teenagers?

Child soldiers.

Athena rubs her face. Pinches the bridge of her nose in an attempt to stave off some wretched incoming headache. She knows it's dehydration from all the drinking last night. Water would be a good idea.

Father Bill points to the passenger cars in front and back. "Troops are stationed in every car, obviously. In addition to that, there are mounted guns on the roofs—three .50-caliber M2 Brownings, two in the front, one in the back. The nine others are variety of light machine guns atop the more central cars. M249s and M60s." He turns to Michelle. "Not that you'll need to worry about that." He smiles.

Michelle doesn't smile at first. Her eyes remain fixed on the diesel-powered Bulldozer. The guns. The kids. The fuel. The barbed wire. The spikes.

Damned thing must look like a nightmare engine to her.

Mark puts his hands on her shoulders. Turns her. Wraps his arms around her in a hug and pats her back.

She snaps herself back to reality. Nods. Gives Father Bill a quick smile. "Just. . .show me to the kitchen." She looks to Athena. Lifts the hand-crank radio with a little smirk.

Father Bill gestures to the young redhead. "My daughter Emma will take you there. It's the second car. Emma?"

The young redhead slings her rifle. Holds out her hand for Michelle to shake.

The pregnant brunette does. "Nice to meet you. I'm Michelle."

"Nice to meet you as well." Though she doesn't sound convincing.

When they're outta earshot, Mark says, "Your daughter. . .is a very serious girl."

Father Bill chuckles. Grins at the older redhead. "Takes a bit more after her mother in that regard, I think. Emma doesn't want to chauffeur people around—"

"She wants to fight," the older redhead says. Thrusts her hand out toward Mark and Athena. "I'm Colette."

Mark introduces himself.

As does Athena.

Colette *seems* a hair less hostile now, but not much warmer. She says, "These days, you need to be a fighter if you're going to survive at all." She eyeballs Athena. "Don't you agree?"

Athena licks her lips. Cocks her hips. Sucks on her teeth. Stares Colette down. "I fuckin somehow *do* something to you I'm not aware of?"

"I'm worried about what you *might* do. What kind of corruption you might bring to my family."

"With what? With who?" Athena throws her hands out. "I got my car. I got my guns. I got *smokes*. I got *whiskey*. My goal?" She points west. "All I wanna do is get to the redwoods before the clock on my cancer chimes.

"Save the world. Make it Catholic. Run your fuel. Keep your kids." Athena shakes her head. "It doesn't *matter* to me. I ain't here to get in your way."

Athena remembers in this instant why she hates talking.

Colette doesn't back down.

Got a lotta guns behind her, after all.

She hisses. "You're a smoker. You're a boozer." Colette looks Athena up and down. "You're a blasphemer and probably a whore. Just look at all that leather. You awful easterners are all the same— taking advantage of the world's new lawlessness for all sorts of perversions."

Father Bill puts a heavy hand on Colette's shoulder. Squeezes. "Colette. . . ." His voice is deep and serious, but gentle in its attempt to calm. "This isn't what we do."

Mark does precisely the opposite and looks around for a way to extricate himself from a situation involving an explosive, violent Athena. Cuz Mark knows what happens.

It ain't fear so much as an understanding of the inevitable: Athena kills people.

But Athena knows this'll be a short goddamn trip if she lashes out now.

Yeah, she's reactionary as hell. Callous. Mean. A bitch.

What she ain't is stupid.

She balls her fists. "Only man I've been with for more than twenty years was my husband." Then relaxes em. Sighs. "Only thing I'm doing is trading our services for transit." She crosses her arms. "I'm the best driver. The best mechanic. The best shooter. Mark's the best doctor." The fact that he couldn't save her leg flashes across her mind. "The pregnant girl, Michelle, she can fight—even if you don't want her to. We're travelers here, relying on you. That's all."

Mark arches his eyebrows at Athena. Doesn't say anything. But steps forward to stand with her.

Father Bill nods. Squeezes Colette's shoulder again. "I believe we have a moral obligation to help." He looks to Colette.

She takes in a big lungful of air. Exhales slow. "I'm. . .sorry. Things have been difficult for us recently and that's gotten into my head."

Athena keeps her mouth shut. Posture neutral.

Colette says, "We're happy to have you onboard."

Mark clears his throat. "Which train car is the infirmary? Not to sound like a dick, but if you've lost so many people to the Wraiths— and you still have wounded who need treatment—shouldn't you get my ass over there to help?" He puts his hands on his hips.

"Of course, of course," Father Bill says. He steps away from Colette. Toward Mark. Gestures the doctor closer. "Have you ever seen a Wraith before?"

Mark shakes his head. "No."

Father Bill shifts his focus to Athena. "You?"

She shakes her head. "Don't even know what the hell a 'Wraith' is."

Father Bill straightens his back. Rubs his forehead. "The name. . .describes their terror well, I'm afraid. They aren't ambushers like most of the other gangs in the wastes. Like the Iron Cross. The Black Dawn. No, the Wraiths are hunters. Generally clad in billowing rags. They prefer their dirt bikes and modified motorcycles to any other vehicle. It gives them that ghostly appearance. When they make a kill, they send scrap trucks out to collect. Big four-by-fours." He waves to Athena and Mark.

They follow.

Athena says to Father Bill, "You can't outrun dirt bikes?"

"The Bulldozer is not a speed demon. It's meant to haul, not win races." He talks and walks toward the back of the train. Says, "They don't use guns. They use crossbows and bladed weapons."

Father Bill steps into the first double-decker after the freight cars. Makes a right and plods down a short set of stairs into the infirmary. Both floors have been cleared of passenger seating. Instead are installed hospital beds and health monitoring devices stolen from clinics. Gurneys strapped and snapped into place using old seatbelts. There's room for twenty-four beds.

All of em are stained.

Six of em have unconscious patients. Four teens. Two older. Tubes of saline run from their arms. A young nurse waltzes between all of em. Girl in her early twenties. She checks their vitals. Seems harried and grim.

Father Bill gestures to the comatose Trakers. "If you get hit by an arrow or cut with one of their blades—and don't die—this is what happens." He frowns. His voice is low. Solemn. "You scream and scream until we can get enough morphine into you to knock you out." He groans. Genuinely sad, it sounds, about the state of his troops. "This, Hellcat. . .I need competent fighters. I need them very badly."

Mark steps farther into the car. Gets near the nurse. Says, "When was the attack?"

The nurse locks eyes with Mark. Studies him for a second. Looks over to Father Bill.

Father Bill nods.

The nurse says, "Thirty-six hours ago or so. Wraiths hit us hard as we were coming out of Chicago."

Mark motions with his hand. "You mind?" Slips between the nurse and the patient in front of him. Lifts the stained white sheet up.

This guy was hit in the upper thigh. Something mean got him. The wound, though covered with gauze, is swollen. A blown up balloon of flesh that leaks red and yellow.

Mark pulls back the gauze. Hisses between his teeth when he sees the damage.

A necrotic puncture in the skin. Brown, dead muscle under that. As though the underlying tissues—even while they expanded—didn't want to get near. . .whatever it was that drilled a hole in the soldier.

In other places along the thigh, swelling has caused the healthy muscle to split the skin. Resulting in nauseating tears of flesh with bright red muscle underneath.

Mark doesn't look at the nurse. He keeps his eyes on the patient. "What are you giving him in the IV?"

"A saline solution and antibiotics. I'm trying to keep the heartrate up." She crosses her arms. Like she's half-expecting him to give her shit about the treatments.

He doesn't. "Okay, that's a good first step to stabilization." He cranes his neck to see Father Bill. "I'm gonna need access to all your medical supplies. And I need to know if you've got antivenin in good supply. Has to be fresh. Any CroFab made in the last thirty months or so."

Father Bill says, "Cro. . . Of course. Anything to get these people back on their feet. I don't know if we have antivenin. Why would we need it?"

"Antivenin is antivenom. Doesn't this look familiar to you?" He points to the wound. "Albeit much more extreme?"

Father Bill squints. Breathes through his nose.

Mark says, "This is a poisonous snake bite writ large. The Wraiths are coating their weapons in, probably, rattlesnake venom."

"If we get CroFab, can you save my soldiers?"

Mark doesn't say anything. He just moves on to the next Wraith victim and sees the same type of wound over and over and over.

A poisoned nightmare.

* * *

Two hours later, they've moved everyone and all the supplies onto the train. Left a separate contingent of Trakers at the walled-off square to hold the fort. Keep away the insect swarms. Keep any muties at bay.

Ten healthy soldiers hold Indianapolis for the Trakers.

The Bulldozer itself pulls away from the station while Athena waits in the Hellcat.

On account of the elevated tracks in downtown, she's gotta regroup with everyone across the White River. To the west. Where the Bulldozer will actually be on solid ground again.

Another kid in another backhoe move concrete blocks so she can leave the Amtrak camp. Head north a bit. Turn the Hellcat left onto Maryland Street. Roll as it turns into Washington Street. Over the bridge. Over the water. Left again on Harding Street.

And just south a bit waits the Bulldozer. A freight car coupled to the ass of the train—the new last car, just for her—is open at the side. Two yellow ramps are placed down.

Athena guides the Hellcat up into it. After some careful maneuvering, she's got her vehicle parked. Emergency brake *on*.

Back of this big, segmented metal worm.

She's the fresh ass.

A couple of young Trakers rush in to restrain the Dodge with thick cambuckle tie downs threaded through hooks in the walls. The equivalent of seatbelts for cars themselves instead of the passengers inside.

The Bulldozer lurches forward.

Athena hears the engine at the front chug. Vibrations shudder and shake over the train's length.

She takes a wide-legged stance. Like she used to on the subways in New York City. Waits till she feels the rhythm of movement. Walks forward toward the door. Grabs the latch. Pulls it open.

There's no real walkway between cars. It's two ever-shifting plates to stand on. Corrugated platforms that shimmy back and forth and sometimes bump into one another.

She steps out onto it.

The tracks and the ground rush by in a blur beneath her.

She thinks: *Holy fuck. We're really going now.*

She steps across. Pounds on the door to the next car.

A Traker on the other side stares at her. Refers to some ledger she's got in her hands. Then unlocks the door.

Athena walks into a cramped passenger car turned storeroom. Boxes of supplies. All the crap they were loading before.

She stomps wide-legged through. Between the canned food. Water. Ammo.

Repeats the door-knocking and the clearance process through three more cars. A barracks. Another barracks. Another supply car. Then the infirmary.

When she gets inside, Father Bill is in tears.

Colette is pissed.

Emma ain't doing much of anything except hold a corpse's hand in her own.

Five of the patients are dead. Sheets up over their head.

The sixth is missing her arm.

Mark sees Athena. Meets her gaze. Shakes his head.

His voice is plagued by guilt. Lilting. Hitting deep notes in whispers. "CroFab antivenin has a shelf-life of thirty months. Even if we'd had some. . . ." He wipes his bloody hands on his flannel shirt. "After a certain time period. . .with the tissue dying and necrosis setting in. . .amputation is the only option." He blinks. "Otherwise, the merciful thing to do is up the morphine dosage until they just. . .go to sleep for good."

Emma frowns. She releases the corpse's hand. "So we get put down like dogs."

Mark stares at the floor. "It's a quiet death."

As though that makes it any better.

Yeah. We're really going.

We're really going into more death and dismay.

For a moment, though, Athena's glad one of her thighs is metal. Gonna be hard to get hit with an arrow there.

She doesn't offer any words to anyone.

She stomps through the car. Forward. Toward the engine.

10.

Athena watches Michelle stir four jumbo pots of Chef Boyardee ravioli.

The Dapper brothers and Jimi Hendrix's "All Along the Watchtower" pour from the little speakers on the hand-crank radio.

The Hellcat driver says, "They've literally got you pregnant and barefoot in the kitchen."

"I took my shoes off cuz my feet are killing me." Michelle sniffs the food. Leaves her big spoon in the mix. "Do you have *any idea* what it's like to be this pregnant? All the weight on your back and feet?"

Athena remembers the baby she never got to have with David.

Shakes her head.

Clears her throat.

Refrains from lighting a smoke.

Michelle leans back. Twists to work some kinks outta her back. "It's. . .I want my baby to be all right. I want my baby to be able to enter this world with as many options and strengths as possible. As safely as possible. But—" She grins at Athena. "A big part of me just wants this bastard out of my belly."

She waddles. Turns. Leans back against a beige counter. "I'm farting, like, all the time. My tits feel like hot bowls of chili. My feet are nightmares of lava and pain—"

Athena holds up a hand. "Yeah. *Yeah.* I hear you."

Michelle watches Athena for a second. "Why're you here, really." Her eyes swivel and focus on the barbwired windows.

The grey landscape slips by outside. Suburban houses blend into each other along with the poisoned trees and dusty grass.

Athena absent-mindedly checks her 1911. Her sawed-off shotgun. Shrugs. "I don't know." She sighs. "I really don't. I feel like. . . ."

"What?" Michelle rolls her tongue around in her mouth. "You need a fuckin friend all of the sudden?"

Athena frowns.

It is that and it isn't.

Athena would rather have never met Mark. Would rather have never met Michelle. Easier when you don't have anyone at all, these days. Just live for yourself. Take the losses. Charge forward. To hell with everyone anyway.

Now Athena, Mark, and Michelle are locked into a particular trajectory. Together.

"I. . .don't think you should be in the kitchen," Athena says. "I think you should be slinging lead. Killing."

Michelle chuckles. Shakes her head. Goes back to the pot of fake food and stirs with her spoon. "It's hard to be violently killed while cooking. I think this is solid step in the right direction." She points to her belly. "Simple work since I have other things on my mind."

Athena continues to fight her smoker's urge to light up. "That ain't even cooking. It's heating." She fidgets. Cracks her knuckles. Unsure what to do with her hands.

Michelle flaps a hand. "Fine, whatever. It's heating and trying to make sure this food doesn't burn. I'm uselessly babysitting canned crap. That what you wanna hear?"

It ain't. Quite. She'd rather hear Michelle say that this was busywork for a woman and *mean it* and then storm off to one of the gun turrets and show Father Bill how to get some killing done so that no more child soldiers get venom death sentences.

But that's not gonna happen. At least, it doesn't seem that way.

Athena's not sure how to tactfully bail on this conversation. So she doesn't bother trying.

She just walks away. Passes through another coupling section.

Another young face examines her. Then approves her.

She steps into the cramped engine.

Space is in short supply. There's only room for one person to walk back and forth from the cab. The walls are all fat pipes and machinery. The massive engine takes up the majority of the car and runs all the way from the back to the cab. Pale beige but with the paint falling off, exposing the darker metal beneath. It's loud enough to damage someone's hearing. The vibrations are strong enough to shake Athena's guts.

The engine car is effectively just housing for the fuckoff big diesel beast.

Sodium lights overhead cover everything in a funky light orange glow.

The car opens up a little in the cab. There are two seats to the far left and right that sit in front of a huge wraparound control console. Thing's got as many buttons and levers as a goddamn spaceship. The windows are high up—you have to stand to see through em. Even still, visibility ain't great on account of the protective scrap metal strategically welded in place to cut down on the odds of a crossbow bolt hitting the driver in the face.

Father Bill's there. Both literally and figuratively keeping the Trakers on track. He glances over his shoulder. Acknowledges Athena without saying anything. Returns his eyes to driving. A rosary wobbles from a hook to his right.

The view from here does illustrate why the Bulldozer can't blaze across the landscape at one-fifty, though: There's all kinds of shit on the rails. Dust, of course. Debris and detritus that's been thrown around by the storms.

Athena watches a small screen that shows a fisheye view of what's directly in front of the train.

What the Bulldozer lacks in speed it makes up for in pure brute force.

Father Bill doesn't blink or slow as they approach a tree fallen across the tracks. He keeps the throttle steady. A scalloped cowcatcher attached to the engine's nose scoops up the wood. Father Bill punches a button on the dash. An industrial blade emerges from the center. Chews up the log. Splinters it. The pieces tumble away from each side. They bounce and kick up dust.

The Traker leader smiles quietly to himself.

Athena can imagine how satisfying that's gotta be.

She sits in the left seat. Leans back. Digs a pack of cigarettes outta her jacket. Looks over to Father Bill. "You mind?"

He studies her for a moment. Eyes flit between her cigarettes and the rails ahead. He points to a slim door near the back of the cab. "Crack that open." He pauses. "And give me one."

Athena stands. Leans outside the cab. Pulls the door in. Can't use it to get out. The doorway doesn't actually go anywhere. It's all blocked off with more scrap. But it allows wind to rush into the train. Great gusts and *wooshes* of air.

She covers her Bic with her hands. Lights her stogie. Enjoys the rush of nicotine even though it hasn't been all that long since her last one. She sits back in the seat. Plucks a second cigarette from her pack. Hands that and the lighter to Father Bill.

He takes it with one hand. The other still on one of the many controls on the console. Father Bill pops the cig in his mouth. Lights it. Tosses the Bic back to Athena.

After a long drag, he says, "I used to smoke like a damn chimney when I was at the seminary."

Athena watches him. Watches the grey world go by outside.

He breathes smoke. "I was not the best priest in the world." He grunts. "Then the world was over, and I found that I was the *only* priest in the world."

Athena sniffs. "I think that makes you, *de facto*, y'know, the best priest."

Father Bill chuckles. "I suppose." He stares out the front windows. Squints at something in the distance Athena can't see. Says, "Which would make Colette the best nun."

Athena arches her eyebrows. That explains her shitty reactions. A goddamn nun.

He says, "It seemed like the right thing to do. For us to start the world again. Procreate. Save the human race. That's about when I switched from preaching the word of God to preaching the word of engineering."

Athena watches the smoke curl from her cigarette. "You're just giving a world of chaos and pain more to eat." She flicks ash onto the ground.

He doesn't respond.

She says, "How do you even manage these kids with the germ? The radiation out here? Where did they come from?"

Father Bill eyes her. "For someone who works very hard to not care, you're asking some serious questions."

Athena shakes her head. "Just wanna know what the fuck the situation is. These can't all be your children." She squints at him. "Unless you and Colette have some new way of doing things."

Father Bill scratches his cheek. Chuckles again. "No, no. That part of it is the same as it always has been."

Athena grunts.

Father Bill continues: "Most of the children here are the sons and daughters of other Trakers. Service like this is mandatory—a rite of passage. It's one of the many reasons it breaks my heart when they're harmed. Others are orphans we've found along the way. We feed them and train them. They're free to go, of course, but they prefer to stay with the family." He shrugs. "Better to be in the company of others. Where it's not so lonely.

"As for the germ and the radiation. . .I'm afraid I don't know. One of our theories is that the constant background radiation has killed off both the cancer and the germ—though it may lead to tumors later. Of course, without a highly-skilled medical staff, we don't even know if the children *have* cancer. And the only way we know they *don't* have the germ is because they aren't *dead*." He pauses. Catches himself before he gets angry. Clears his throat.

Athena clicks her tongue. Takes a pull from the cigarette. "Yeah." She stands. "Catch you around, Padre." She starts off toward the cab's rear.

Father Bill shouts over his shoulder. "I'm going to need you on a mounted gun before we get to Chicago. About five hours from now. We scared the Wraiths off before, but that doesn't mean they won't come back at us."

Athena nods. "The doctor and the pregnant woman can shoot too."

"Uh huh." Father Bill's mouth ain't smirking or smiling anymore. And the humor's gone from his voice. "Don't take this the wrong way, but the world needs doctors and babies more than it needs drivers right now. I'm not putting them in the line of fire."

They stare at each other. The priest's words hang in the air.

Athena says, "Enjoy the smoke." She turns. Flicks her cigarette out the open cab door. Leaves the engine.

Yeah.

It ain't that what Father Bill said was *wrong*. Or even particularly hurtful.

But Athena'll be goddamned if she's considered *expendable* by these fuckers.

Which she is.

She makes her way through the train cars. Doesn't stop to check in on Mark or Michelle. She sticks to the upper floors specifically to avoid em. Got no desire to talk to anyone at all.

Been doing too much of that lately. And where's it gotten her? So fuck it.

She heads to the locked-down Hellcat. Pops the trunk. Grabs a bottle of booze. Some funky whiskey she's barely ever heard of. Jefferson's Ocean? Whatthefuckever. She pops the top. Takes a healthy pull.

Thinks: *Can't even smoke next to my own fuckin car cuz of all the crude oil in here and I'm too pissed off for my own good.*

Athena cracks her neck. Takes the bottle with her as she enters the adjacent train car. A barracks of some kind. The seating all switched out for bunk beds.

She stomps up the stairs to the second level. Points at one of the child soldiers up there. A black girl. Says, "Mounted gun?"

The girl tilts her head up. Toward a hatch with a rotating handle. "Through there." Her voice not as stern or mean as the others. But still no-nonsense.

Athena reaches for the release. Spins it. Pulls the hatch lid down. A small ladder is built into the side that hangs toward her. She climbs it, whiskey still in hand.

The mounted gun is part of a domed-in area. A three foot-by-three foot igloo made from more rusty scrap metal. There's just enough room overhead for Athena to kneel behind the machine gun. The only open section is the one the .50 caliber Browning's barrel faces out from. Looks like it can fire in a ninety-degree arc.

It's impressive.

Athena plops her ass down on a couch cushion. Used to be a floral pattern but wear and weathering have worn it down. Lucky enough that the thing still has some padding.

She leans back against the metal dome. Lifts the whiskey to her lips. Enjoys the hot, bitter feeling. The rush of warmth to her cheeks.

David.

She thinks about David.

Lights a cigarette. Watches the breeze catch the smoke and throw it away from the train. It's nice in spite of the weaponry attached to Athena's thighs. The .45 pistol. The 12-gauge shotgun.

Athena smiles while the whiskey burns.

She remembers. . .Remembers one anniversary when he couldn't afford roses. Couldn't even afford fuckin flowers.

So David walked around New York. All the little gardens.

And he picked dandelions. Long-stemmed weeds with a bitter yellow smell.

They were living. . .She doesn't remember where they were living. Probably Brooklyn. Maybe Queens.

Athena only remembers the bouquet of weeds.

The vase she found for em.

The fact that they *mattered*. Cuz at least he tried.

She smokes. Drinks.

Watches the trails of dust behind the Bulldozer.

Waits for some epiphany to occur to her. Some deep thought between the nostalgia and the inebriation.

It never comes.

So she drinks a bit more and falls asleep in the rust.

Watching dust.

11.

Klaxons.

Athena's legs kick out involuntarily. Hit the base of the metal dome.

Some weird alarm. A low pitch and thrum followed by the high notes of a whale song.

Between the howl of the alarm is a shitload of automatic gunfire.

She shakes her head.

Fuck was she dreaming about?

David.

Children.

The redwoods.

Athena blinks.

The dust trails behind the train ain't the same.

She gets to her feet. Crouches. Squints.

Sees small figures on bikes with low profiles. Wraiths. They peel out from behind suburban Chicago homes. Through overgrown backyards. They jump decrepit fences. Two or three dozen of the insane bastards. Engines on their bikes together a chorus of angry insects. Their tattered clothing billows in the wind as they surge forward in the orange glow of the evening. Whatever the hell they're wearing—masks, something that covers their entire faces—the eyes burn yellow.

Athena sniffs. "That ain't fuckin creepy at all."

Voices below her sound off:

"There's already someone there."

"Who. *Who?*"

Sounds like Colette asking the questions. The young black girl answering.

"The angry lady. The Hellcat."

"If she doesn't start killing, she's out. I'll tell Father Bill that myself."

Athena mutters, "Motherfucker."

She checks the gun's belt feed. Yanks back the charging handle on the M2 Browning. Looks down the iron sights. Brings it to bear on one quick figure to her right. A dirt bike. The tires throw up dust in pinwheels. Yellow eyes glower at her, unblinking.

Athena grips the spade handles. Presses the V-shaped butterfly trigger with her thumbs. Sends big fat bullets to say hello. The M2 *chugga chugga*s in short bursts. Rounds pepper the ground around the dirt bike's front wheel. One connects. Shatters the tire and the spokes. The bike stops dead. The rider gets thrown end over end. He lands in a tangled heap near the tracks. Legs and arms bent in awkward directions.

There's one outta. . .Thirty.

That she can see.

Athena opts to be less stingy with the lead-slinging. She opens up on every yellow-eyed glow that crosses her line of sight. Doesn't hit all of em, but she sure makes em scatter.

The *pings* and *pangs* of crossbow bolts hitting the outside of her dome tells her she's got their undivided attention.

She keeps the bullets flowing. Heavy metal rain.

Chugga chugga.

Bullet casings chime as they hit the train roof.

A .50-cal round pounds into a Wraith's face. Obliterates everything there. Chunks of the mask fly. The glow dies fast. Flesh. Bone. Brain. A pink mist in the evening air.

His bike teeters and tumbles in the weeds.

Athena punches more holes in another Wraith. Then another. Their bikes and bodies break under the barrage of bullets.

Then she's outta ammo. The big box the belt fed in from now empty.

Athena pops up the M2's bolt cover. Clears the breach. Looks down at another ammo box. Grunts. Shoves the empty box away. She starts to feed a fresh belt into the Browning.

The Wraiths all around surge closer. Swarm.

She watches em weave between tracer rounds from the Traker's other guns. Bright streaks of red and green light to her right and left. Lasers in the dying day.

Athena gets another belt fed into the gun. Unleashes high-caliber hell on Wraiths who've gotten way too fuckin close in the short period she wasn't shooting. A few are within twenty feet of the last freight car—where the Hellcat is.

Not so good.

A growl claws its way up from Athena's throat. She punishes those nearest her vehicle. Drills their heads and torsos with bullets.

One of the bikes explodes in a glorious fireball of death. The burning gasoline engulfs two more riders. They fall. Burn. Ignite the dry grass they land in. Twist and spasm as their clothing melts on em.

Athena thinks: *Must've been a spark in just the right place plus a gas leak.*

Whatever. She'll take it.

Ten more Wraiths fall to her wrath.

Then she's outta bullets again.

Even with their numbers dwindling and tribe members getting shot to shit, they show no sign whatever of backing off. Makes Athena curious about em. She wonders if they're really that desperate or stupid to get *all* of themselves killed in this attempt.

She gets the *why* of it. The train is a helluva target. It's got food. Medical supplies. All that fuel. Guns. Ammo. Healthy breeding stock in the form of a couple dozen teenage Catholics.

It's a pure fuckhead perspective, but she gets it.

Which's quietly worrying in itself.

Athena shakes her head. Feeds the final belt into the gun. Fast.

But not fast enough.

Three Wraiths make it to the freight car. They match speed with it. Steady themselves. Grab for the handrails where they can. They're tight enough against the side of the train that Athena doesn't have a shot.

Fuck.

She scrambles outta the dome. Squeezes by the big machine gun. Fights to keep her footing on the roof of the train as it rattles under her. She stomps toward the freight car. Pauses at the gap between it and this last passenger car. Then throws herself over. Lands with a grunt on its red roof.

The other Wraiths hold their crossbow fire.

Probably don't wanna nail one of their own.

Athena draws her 1911. Peaks over the side. Sees one Wraith pull himself up. He lets his bike topple and skitter away.

His yellow eyes snap up to look at her.

She puts a .45 slug in his forehead.

His body tumbles. Limp. His feet slip under the train wheels. They chew him into little gory chunks.

She hears the *slap* of a glove hitting metal behind her. Whips around. Sees another Wraith working his way up the other side.

His masked head pops up. Some kind of plastic rebreather or filter over his mouth. Yellow illuminated goggles above that. A plastic helmet. Long strips of tattered clothing attached to that.

They're raggedy people.

Athena kicks the Wraith's face. Her boot cracks the goggles. His hands flail.

He falls.

Someone gets Athena in a bear hug from behind. Muscular arms wrap around her own. Pin her hands to her sides. She struggles. Grunts. Yells.

She can hear the Wraith's heavy breathing. The strange echoing sound is makes through his mask. He smells like mold. Decay.

A fourth Wraith clambers up over the edge. Blade in his hands. A rusty machete.

He charges toward Athena.

She roars. Twists her wrist. Fires the 1911 three times. Down. One of the bullets splatters the bear-hugging Wraith's toes. He howls. She elbows him in the gut. Brings the 1911 up in a flash. Fires twice into the machete-wielding Wraith. Both rounds pound his chest.

He drops to his knees.

Athena puts another in his head to be sure. Ejects the empty mag from her Springfield Armory pistol. Stuffs it into her jacket. Holsters the gun.

She turns back to the Wraith howling over his ruined toes. The bastard curled in a raggedy ball on his side.

Athena lifts her right robotic foot. Stomps down with a furious shout.

She crushes the Wraith's skull. Kicks his leaky dead body over the side. Into the dust.

Someone below in the freight car shouts. Then there's gunfire.

Athena gets low. Lies on her belly. Hears a crossbow bolt sail by her head. She ignores it. Crawls to the side of the cargo container. Peers down.

Two Wraiths have managed to get a sliding door open.

They're inside. Fighting with children over the spoils.

And the Hellcat.

Athena holds onto the edge of the roof. Throws her legs over. Swings into the car.

One teenager is dead on her back. Thirteen or so. Her throat slit and still pouring dark blood between spent shell casings. Her body's partially unclothed. Pale thighs exposed. Khaki jumpsuit slashed and torn. Like the Wraiths wanted to rape her, but got interrupted.

Interrupted by the second teenager they're tearing at. Ripping at. It's the young black girl who pointed Athena to the mounted gun before the Hellcat driver passed out in a drunken stupor.

She's a fighter. Won't give up. She shouts and tries to free herself. Kicks at their knees and shins. Gnashes her teeth at their fingers if they get too close.

Athena runs at em like a linebacker. Lowers her shoulder and hits the closest one in the kidney. He *oofs* from the impact. Gets thrown forward. Hits a skeletal metal container holding a supply of crude.

The second grabs for Athena.

She frees her sawed-off shotgun. Can't shoot the imprecise scattergun in case some pellets hit the girl. So she whips him across the face with it. Breaks the mask. Jabs his head with the hollow barrels. The goggles break. Their yellow glow turns red as blood dribbles over em.

The other Wraith collects himself. Pulls a knife. Nowhere near the black girl now.

He gets a brain full of buckshot from Athena.

A third Wraith appears from behind the Hellcat. Apparently he was trying to break into it. Couldn't get passed the metal sheets that cover the windows. He scuttles across the hood. Knife drawn. Yellow glow locked on Athena.

She gives him the second shell of shot from the gun.

Pellets rip through his rags. Scramble his guts.

He falls facedown. Clutching his stomach as gore rains from him.

Athena breaks open the sawed-off. Plucks out the used shells. Replaces em. "Don't touch the fuckin car."

The Wraith she bloodied lunges for her again. Knife already in a downward arc.

She blocks his wrists with the shotgun. Blade mere inches from her face.

The Wraith fights with a mad, blind bloodlust.

Poisoned point of his blade getting closer. Closer.

Athena growls. Roars as her muscles strain.

The Wraith's body spasms. He makes a gurgling sound. The fight leaves him. His ragged, echoed breathing stops.

His body drops.

The black young girl in the torn khaki jumpsuit holds a bloody blade up. One of the Wrath's own poison daggers.

Athena looks at the body of her fallen foe.

There's a neat, crimson hole at the base of his neck.

The girl with the blade breathes heavy. Her brown eyes meet Athena's blues. She nods once.

Athena returns the gesture. Works to catch her breath.

A crossbow bolt pierces the leather on her right leg. *Clang*s off the metal of her prosthetic underneath.

The girl cocks her head at Athena.

A heartbeat later a bolt plunges into her chest.

Athena drops to one knee. Pulls the 1911. Slams a fresh mag in. Squints and scans outside to locate the motherfucker who shot the girl.

But she can't see anything.

The scenery blows by too fast.

The sounds of dirt bike engines fade.

Combat seems to have slowed. Become less frenzied and mad. Gunfire she hears from the Bulldozer's mounted guns is more sparse. Only a few pops here and there.

Could be a lack of things to shoot at.

Could be a lack of Trakers to pull their triggers.

Athena rushes to the girl's side. Yanks the bolt from her flesh. Presses her palms against the bloody hole to stem any blood loss. Gives up on that as crimson coats her hands. She tears a strip of cloth from the teen's khaki jumpsuit. Bunches it up. Presses it down. Maneuvers the girl's hands so she can deal with it herself.

The girl's already suffering from the poison and the wound. Her breathing is more labored. Shallow but strained. At the same damn time, the flesh on her chest swells. Becomes discolored.

Athena groans. Stands. Grunts as she pulls the teen to her feet. Then hefts the girl onto her shoulders.

She carries the barely-breathing girl through the barracks. Between bunks. Between other kids who've been bloodied. Other kids who stink of sweat and cordite.

They watch the Hellcat with awe and fear. They stay outta her way.

Till she gets to the medical bay.

She points to Mark. Shouts. "Poisoning."

The girl Athena carries ain't the only casualty. Of the dozens of beds, most are occupied by teenagers who've been injured in some way. They moan. Weep from the pain. Cry out for Mark and his nurse.

Mark nods to Athena. Points to an empty bed.

Athena lays the girl down.

The doctor checks her pulse. Listens for her heartbeat. He yells to his nurse. "We gotta get this swelling in her chest down *now*." He brushes by Athena. Tells her, "I'll do what I can, but I'm gonna need space."

Athena watches the girl for a moment.

The teen's eyes start to glaze over, but she's able to mouth a whisper that Athena can't hear and doesn't follow.

What the girl can't say is irrelevant.

The Hellcat driver nods. That in itself is the most solid acknowledgment she'll ever adorn a random stranger with.

Understanding. Mutual appreciation.

She turns. Marches out toward the train's engine. Where she wants to find Father Bill and tell him he's a goddamn moron.

This child soldier shit.

If there's some grand patriarchal society in Houston. . . . Some buncha rich goddamn oilmen. . . . Those are the people who should be fighting to trade their crude. Not some kids with no idea how the worlds works. How downright *mean* this all is now.

Boys and girls who don't yet even know their own bodies subjected to war and rape.

Athena seethes.

Before she realizes it, she's marched through the passenger cars. The freight cars. The kitchen. The other barracks. And she's right outside the engine room.

She feels the sudden weight of all the eyes that watched her walk.

The eyes that're still on her.

Her righteousness falters.

She doesn't wanna be the center of attention.

Doesn't wanna be a symbol of anything at all.

She takes a deep breath.

Colette opens the door. Eyeballs Athena. "We've already heard." Her body blocks the passageway. "The others passed it up the line." Colette looks to the ground. "What you've done for Nadege is. . .remarkable. We are so sadly resigned to the idea that a Wraith wound means death, but. . . ." She looks to Athena again. "You've given her hope—both through your actions and through the doctor."

Colette lifts a small black duffel bag up. Offers it to Athena.

Says, "You're going to need this on the other side of Chicago.

Consider it a gift, if you want. All we ask is that you stay with us. We need someone like you."

Athena sniffs. Grunts. Takes the duffel and throws its strap over her shoulder. It's got some weight. Some bulk.

She wants to tell Colette and her hubby Father Bill to get fucked, but still needs the ride.

Colette says, "We're close enough to Union Station and the fort there that the Wraiths won't bother us for a while. You can get some rest if you need it." She arches her eyebrows. No doubt smells the booze wafting off the Hellcat driver. "We usually spend a few hours in Chicago to shift supplies and recuperate." She shrugs. Still doesn't make room for Athena to pass through. Obviously doesn't intend to.

Athena realizes this is as pleasant as the nun is gonna get.

Realizes, also, that the teenagers watching her are gonna be disappointed. She ain't gonna provide em with a big display.

Even if she wants to dethrone Father Bill and Colette and put these kids to work in some way that ain't just for the benefit of oil barons and bullshit artists who wanna act like they're doing the noble thing.

Nope.

Athena is gonna do what gets her closer to her goal.

So Athena holds pat. Grunts again. Turns tail and heads back to the Hellcat. Weight of Colette's gift on her shoulders.

The teenagers keep their eyes on her.

All the way back to the Dodge.

Athena frowns at the bloodstain where the young girl had her throat slit in the freight car.

The body's gone. There's a boy near there now. He mops at the spot.

Athena unlocks her car. Slips into the driver's seat. Keeps the metal shutters up so nobody can see in. Dumps the duffel in the passenger seat. Shuts the door. Waits for some of her adrenaline to bleed off.

She waits. Thinks.

Rubs her face.

Turns on the radio.

The Dapper brothers are playing Spirit's "I Got A Line On You."

Makes her smile for about three minutes. Then she's depressed as hell again.

She heads back to the mounted gun. Reclaims her bottle of whiskey. Remarkably unbroken. She gets back in the Hellcat. Reclines in the driver's seat.

The radio's shifted over to a Carly Simon song. She doesn't know the name of it. Something about thinking about the days to come or some shit.

After a couple pulls from the bottle, Athena opens up the duffel bag Colette gave her. Finds a fat, single-barrel grenade launcher inside. An M79. She knew old fogies at her bar—Vietnam vets—who referred to it as a "thumper" cuz of the noise it made when it fired. A solid thud. Another guy called in a "blooper," but "thumper" is a bit more dignified.

And now the Trakers has given one to her.

Cuz they want her to be some Wraith-killing hero.

Hard not to view the present—Athena's killing prowess dutifully displayed—as a way of saying, "Here. Have fun with the boom booms. Pretend not to notice all deadly flaws in our plans. Also, be quiet about em."

Athena chuckles. Drinks some more. Lights a cigarette inside her car, in spite of all the crude around.

She smokes.

Overhears new guards outside in the freight car wonder if the girl she carried to Mark is even gonna make it through the night.

Athena grunts.

Drinks some more.

Smokes some more.

She'd fall asleep if she wasn't so jacked up on adrenaline.

12.

Chicago Union Station is a behemoth of a transit hub. An icon of the Midwest. Its beauty and enormity and architectural grandeur are accented by limestone facades. Tall Corinthian columns.

None of which Athena gives a shit about.

But, even as a New Yorker spoiled by Grand Central and Penn Station, she's impressed by the expansive track area. A concrete field of stone and steel illuminated by harsh work lights. It's busy with Trakers manning forklifts. Moving supplies.

Armed guards patrol the platforms with assault rifles.

Most of em ain't kids, either. The men and women here have faces weathered by age and the elements. A few sport body armor and carrier rigs over their khaki jumpsuits. They watch Athena with cold eyes. Her back near the mounted fifty. Not in the scrap dome now, but leaning up against it outside.

The Hellcat in her black leather glory.

Murderous. Chain smoking. Half in the bag from whiskey.

She's sure there's a trading outpost here. Has to be. Athena could go mingle. Get intel. Find the Traker bar that undoubtedly exists and swap stories.

Except she doesn't *need* anything right now.

Not supplies.

Not companionship.

She stays at her post on the Bulldozer.

Watches the wounded be carried off. The black girl—Nadege— is still among the living. She and others are checked on by Mark as he escorts em. He consults with whoever's handling medical locally. Older folks. A split between women and men in khakis.

They all nod at each other. Consult some clipboards.

Mark offers em a quick wave.

The dead are dealt with the same way.

But without any consultation.

Don't need to compare notes about fuckin corpses.

Corpses who're replaced moments later by more kids. More fresh meat.

Athena keeps her distance from the whole thing. Watches till she gets kinda bored. Kinda tired. Retreats into the gun dome with her whiskey and smokes and passes out for a couple hours.

* * *

She wakes with a start. Jolted back into consciousness by an air horn. Probably from the Bulldozer itself.

Then there're men and women yelling the same thing over each other: "Night run! Night run!" Not a chant but close.

Father Bill's voice floats out over unseen loudspeakers. "God, we ask that you and your angels guide us and protect us as we travel these dusty rails—"

Athena peaks out from the dome. Cocks an eye. Sees dozens of Trakers with their heads bowed. Their hands together. Fingers intertwined.

"—We pray that no harm comes to we Trakers or the children of Trakers. We pray for safety across the wastes. We pray for safety through the territories of the land whales. We pray for safety through the territories of the Wraiths. Let the western devil never see us. May you watch over us until the earth's days are all past. Amen."

"Amen," echoes through the cavernous underground of Chicago Union Station.

Athena grunts.

The Bulldozer vibrates. Its massive diesel engine cranks to life.

Instead of pulling, it pushes. Bumpers between the cars ram into each other. The train runs backward on the main line till they get a little south. Pass a junction. Where the Bulldozer slows. Chugs. Stops. Chugs again and heads west on a new line.

They rush away from the lights of Union Station.

The night sky above is the darkest Athena has ever seen. Deep black pockmarked by bright stars. Watch long enough, you'll see a shooting star. Maybe a satellite. Without the background illumination from major cities and their electrical grids, it's easy to find all the little astronomical flourishes people once thought were so rare.

The Bulldozer's running lights cast a faint green glow on the tracks. The crumbling apartment blocks. These big buildings that're falling apart brick by brick—right in front of Athena's eyes when the vibrations hit em.

Floodlights at the front, middle and rear of the train focus brilliant beams of white light farther into the decay of Chicago. There are things alive there. Insects. Probably more muties. Athena can only guess. But she sees the stutters of movement.

When they cruise by an enormous park to their right, she sees much more.

At first she thinks the field is filled with a mist or a fog. Looks cloudy. A little bit. . .sparkly. As though there are crystals or particulates in there bouncing light back at the train.

Then long black legs stretch in the shine. Fat pipes attached to an arachnid body the size of a sedan. Eight spindly appendages and their maddeningly big bug centerpiece.

It ain't a fog or a mist she's looking at.

The spider's covered the entire park in webs. A sticky nightmare blanket. The trees are grey-white cones. Other shapes dot the sheet of webbing. Lumps that are human and pet-sized.

Athena thinks launching a couple 40mm grenades into the nest is a great fuckin idea. Torch the sucker. Make use of the boom booms. Though she can't quite square the idea wasting ammo on a bug. Let the Trakers deal with it if they wanna.

This place is their neighborhood, after all.

She lifts her broken binoculars to her eyes. Scans the horizon. Searches for Wraiths giving chase. Finds nothing. Just blackness and deserted buildings.

Could be they really don't wanna deal with Trakers if Union Station is nearby. Could be the urban insects are scary enough to leave the area be.

The density of Chicago proper gives way to endless sprawl of suburbia. Apartments fade into family homes all crammed next to each other block by block. Then it's shopping centers. Sam's Clubs. Home Depots. More trees.

Athena hears something in the distance. A kind of whale song. A deep bassy cry from a titanic beast that swells inside massive unknown lungs.

More spider silk in all those branches. If she watches long enough, she sees the train's lights reflected in their big insect eyes. Glints and hints out in the blackness. Eight pinpricks nestled in the fuzzy face of a speedy carnivore.

The arachnids are a curiosity more than a threat, though.

They seem afraid of the Bulldozer. Apprehensive of the massive machine and the thunderous vibrations it shakes the area with. They haven't gone near the tracks, let alone launched an assault on the train.

The way their arachnid eyes catch the light reminds Athena of the goddamn Wraiths.

She can hear dirt bike engines. Motorcycle engines. Didn't hear em at all when they were in Chicago but she does now. Somewhere far out there, the Wraiths are watching. They're in pursuit.

Gonna be impossible to tell *where* the Wraiths are till they get clear of all these buildings. Or the bastards attack. Either one'll do.

Athena wishes she could spot the glow of their eyes. Send a few rounds their way.

Instead she settles for what constitutes peace and quiet. Has a cigarette. A pull of whiskey.

She makes her way back down into the train. Heads for Michelle's kitchen.

The way her stomach grumbles—pissed at being fed only smoke and booze—grub is a good idea.

Along the way, whispers are added to the stares she gets from teenage Trakers. Mostly mutters she can't hear. Since she never bothered to learn any of the names from the first batch of child soldiers, she has no idea if this is from the new kids or the original ones.

Words like "drunk" and "killer" and "nonbeliever" make it to her ears. As well as words like "Hellcat" and "saved" and "hope."

She's not sure which batch is worse as she passes through into the medical bay. Catches Mark's eye.

He waves to her. Walks up to meet her. "How's it going on your end?"

Athena shrugs. "Pretty much just killing different things than I was before."

Mark takes a deep breath. Nods. Waits for her to ask him how he's doing and realizes quick enough that she won't. He says, "The Wraiths really gave the Trakers a pounding." He frowns at the floor. "I managed to keep most of the kids alive, including the girl you brought back, even though it wasn't easy with limited resources and tools. I can't. . . ." He crosses his arms. His voice becomes a whisper. "Why are they using *kids*?"

"You know why, doc." Athena looks around to see who, if anyone, might be staring at her now. There's a couple nurses nearby. Both seem busy sorting out supplies. "They're young and indoctrinated. Harder to control mature folks who might have an independent thought in their head."

Mark groans. "Jesus Christ."

Athena grunts. "Yeah, exactly the problem."

"What're we gonna do?"

Athena shakes her head. "I'm gonna get some food and keep killing shit till our fare is paid and we drive off outta Denver toward Cali."

Mark considers it. "I guess. . .this isn't any of our business."

"None at all. Just keep doing what you're doing." Athena pushes by Mark. "See ya, doc." Her boots are loud as she stomps up the stairs.

Traker kids back off as she makes her way to the cafeteria. Make room for her to get by. That suits her fine.

Michelle's still cooking. Still barefoot. Still listening to the Dapper brothers' tunes as she tries to keep the contents of four enormous pots from burning.

Wishbone Ash's "Blowin' Free" plays on the radio.

Athena taps Michelle's shoulder.

The pregnant woman turns to her. Sweat all over her face. Cheeks red. She looks at Athena. Doesn't say anything. Seems totally freaked out.

Athena cocks an eye. "What's cooking?"

"There's about forty cans of Dinty Moore fuckin Beef Stew boiling right now." She goes back to stir pot after pot. "I have come to really hate this, by the way. It's hot as hell in here, I still have more cooking to do to feed everyone, and on top of that, things are still trying to kill us everywhere we go."

"That's, uh. . . ." Athena bites her lip. "That's kinda how the world works now. Except we've got an overabundance of food and ammo."

"And creepy little assholes. Emma? The priest's daughter? She's been asking me about my baby. If I was married when I got pregnant. Where the father is now. Am I gonna have the baby baptized." Michelle throws her hands out. "And in my head I'm like, '*Bitch,* I don't need to be having this conversation at all right now.' On top of how shitty I feel anyway, I've done nothing but sniff canned food fumes for like ten hours."

"So take a break." Athena plucks a cigarette from her pack. Doesn't light it but sticks it behind her ear. "Wasn't Father Bill's whole thing about saving babies or whatever? I'm sure someone else can man the stove."

Michelle eyes Athena. Gives her the same look a puppy who wants a treat does. "Could you ask Father Bill for me? I'm *exhausted* and I need to make sure these don't burn."

Athena squints at the pregnant brunette. "You're a grown-ass woman. Ask him yourself."

"I've been on my feet sweating over hot food all day." She stabs at the stew. "And I'm feeling *really fuckin emotional* right now." She holds her hand over her belly.

Athena rubs her face. "Fine." She snaps her fingers at the stew. "I want, like, a whole *bucket* of that crap waiting for me when I get back."

Unbelievable.

Goddamn shit fuck piss.

Granted, Athena does still have more than a few things to say to Colette and Father Bill.

She storms outta the kitchen car. Brushes passed Trakers. A couple try to talk to her. She doesn't acknowledge em. She pounds on the door to the engine cab. Waits. Pounds again.

Colette answers the door. Both eyebrows raised. "Can I help you?"

Athena rolls her tongue around in her mouth. Stares Colette down. "You gotta get the pregnant woman off kitchen duty. Put someone else in there."

The nun nods. Her eyes never unlock themselves from Athena's. "Sure, that's not a problem." She nods again. "Not a problem." She squints at the Hellcat driver. "Is there. . .something else?"

Silence hangs between the two.

Athena doesn't feel any need to fill the void. Says anyway, "Father Bill up there?" She juts her chin over Colette's shoulder.

Colette watches Athena. Another moment of silence. "Yes?" She shakes her head. "Of course he is. He's driving the train. Why?"

"I wanna know how many kids you lost in the last attack." Athena crosses her arms over her chest. "I wanna know if he can talk to the bosses in Houston and get real fighters with real experience out here. The Trakers plan ain't sustainable. You're gonna burn through all your small soldiers."

"From the moment you convinced Father Bill to take you in, you've made it clear that you don't really give a shit about us."

"I don't."

Colette spreads her hands out. "So. . .then. . . .?"

"I ain't here to be your savior. If you get all those kids dead cuz of your inept ability to manage, then it falls to me to protect my investments."

"What investments? What are you *talking about?*"

"The pregnant broad and the doctor." Athena pounds her chest. "They're mine." She points at Colette. "*Your* train just happens to be what'll get me where I need to go."

Colette smiles. "Then it's in your best interest to do what we need you to do."

Athena breathes through her nose. Moves the cigarette from behind her ear to her lips. Lights it. Inhales cancerous smoke.

Colette says, "We've got an electric-diesel engine five feet away with leaky valves and you light a cigarette?"

Athena blows a smoke ring. "You've got several dozen kids who're maybe cancer-and-germ-free and you're using em as battle fodder for the oilmen in Houston—who you've already said you don't like." Athena grins. "Someone's in your pussy, and it ain't the Padre."

"Aww." Colette mocks a blushing girl. "Like I said, I thought you didn't care."

Athena looks around. "Where's your daughter, anyway. Emma. The one who ain't as allergic to the fuckin sun as your ass seems to be."

Colette waggles a mock smile. "Securing provisions, I imagine. She typically mans one of the mounted guns. One of the fifties in front. She's an excellent shot."

Athena taps ash onto the metal floor. "Well, your bitchpup has two things she's gotta do now." She lets her left hand take over the cigarette. Her right hand rest on the butt of her Springfield Armory 1911. "Emma takes over cooking while Michelle rests. . .in my Hellcat."

Colette chuckles. "Is that what all this is about? Sure. Yeah. We'll find someone to stir pots. Anything else?"

"Your bitchpup doesn't ask the pregnant woman any more questions unless she wants a .45 slug through her forehead."

Colette glowers. Doesn't have a response for that.

Athena sniffs. Smokes. Nods.

Says, "Good. We understand each other now."

13.

The Wraiths make their presence known again just before dawn. The sun still hidden below the horizon, but hinting at its emergence with a red and yellow hues that eat away at the blankness of night.

A new engine noise joins the whine of dirt bikes. Something big. Its roars bring images to the forefront of Athena's mind: diesel-guzzling Mack trucks. Ones that look mean. Ones with rams on the front and covered in spikes. Obscene machines from the set of an apocalypse flick.

Above it all is that strange song. Whales calling out in the dust.

Searchlights atop the Bulldozer pan over the landscape. Wherever the train is now, the houses are far more spread out. Fields of dirt and dead crops take the place of suburban sprawl and backyards.

There are scuttling clusters of cat-sized red ants that march in a line between houses they've taken over. Athena watches em from the gun turret. Watches em carry the carcasses of other bugs.

Beetles. Moths with wings five feet wide. Chunks of long worms like ropes or foam pool noodles. Tall mounds pepper the fields. Conical structures as tall as the homes and barns nearby.

Some of the ants flick their antennae as the Bulldozer charges by. But that's the extent of their interest.

Then klaxons sound.

Gunfire erupts along the train.

The dirt bike engines grow louder and louder. Same with those thunderous truck engines.

Athena grips the handles on the machine gun. Swivels left and right. Looks for the telltale glow of the Wraiths' goggles. Finds em. Yellow smears that rush in the darkness.

She opens up. Pours the bullets on. The fifty *chugga chugga*s. Its muzzle flash leaves blooming smudges on Athena's retinas. She blinks. Shakes her head. Keeps shooting.

One of the motherfuckers goes up in a glorious fireball that touches off the dry grass. Gas that leaks from the exploded fuel tank leaves a fiery trail.

Makes Athena glad she requested incendiary rounds.

Every hit is a pretty little firework. A puff of flame that ensures death for the men she's hit. On a few, their clothes go up. Their rags. So they look like insane bipedal matchsticks on motorcycles.

She smiles.

Some kid below her shouts. "Boarding parties! They're using the trucks!"

Which ain't a phrase aimed at Athena. But she leans outta the dome. Looks for em. Whips her head around in the wind. Cuz she can't see shit.

Goddamn trucks are farther up. On both sides of the train.

There's three she can see in the train's floodlights. Troop carriers. Big rigs hauling cargo containers with the roofs chopped off. There's a dozen of the raggedy bastards in each. Geared up.

Three or four of em hold up gas-powered launchers with heavy bolts. Grappling hooks loaded in the front.

Everything happens in a flash.

They fire at the scrap domes on the central cars. Launchers give off a puff of air.

The grappling bolts pierce the domes. The trucks pull away from the Bulldozer. Steel cables from the grappling hooks pull tight. Welds on the domes strain. Groan. Snap.

Two freight car domes tumble free.

The boys inside manning the guns try to turn their M249s to mow down the Wraiths in the trucks nearby.

Not fast enough.

Barrages of crossbow bolts batter their bodies. The boys shudder. Fall. They slam back against the tops of the freight cars.

Wraiths climb ladders inside their trucks. Throw themselves onto the top of the Bulldozer. A few pick up the still-struggling bodies of the boys who were hit.

They toss em over the side.

Seem like they enjoy ruining young lives.

There are screams below.

Someone says, "They're still alive. They're throwing them off the train but those boys were still alive." Panic takes over the voice.

Panic takes over the voices of others.

Athena grunts.

Kids. These dumb assholes really thought using *kids* as soldiers was a good idea.

The bigger question is: How long have these dumb assholes been using kids as cannon fodder? How many post-germ lives have been lost cuz the Houston oligarchy doesn't wanna fight its own fights?

Athena grabs the M79. Slings the black bag of shells over her shoulder. Braces against her scrap dome. Pulls the trigger on the grenade launcher.

It *thump*s.

The 40mm explosive lands at the ass end of the closest truck. Shatters the bodies of the Wraiths engulfed in the boom. Shatters the cargo bed too. Strips of splintered metal flop down. Drag on the ground. Kick up clouds of dust along the tracks.

Athena thumbs the barrel-locking latch to the right. Breaks the gun open like a shotgun. Pulls the smoking spent shell. Chucks that brass away. Stuffs another 40mm shell into the barrel. Snaps it shut.

She *thump*s the fuckin Wraith truck again.

This one doesn't go where she wanted it to. But the result is better.

Instead of landing in the crowd of Wraiths in the cargo bed, it goes boom boom right behind the cab. The front half of the semi ruptures. Flames overtake it. Gas tanks on its sides rupture. Spew burning fuel.

Lit diesel vomits into the rear of the troop carrier. A downpour of fire. The Wraiths in the back get a napalm shower.

They scream and writhe.

The truck slams to a cartoonish halt. Flips when the wheels pop from heat and front bumper of the cab plunges into the ground.

The Bulldozer screams by the wreckage.

Athena loads another grenade. She runs forward. Jumps from her car to the next passenger car roof. Run farther. Legs in a wide stance to maintain her footing.

Wraiths pull themselves up onto the freight cars. A combination of the ladders in the cargo beds and crawling along the cables from the grappling hooks. They climb like frenzied monkeys. Their eyes yellow. The closest few stare at Athena.

She stares back.

Thinks: *Yeah, okay.*

She lets another grenade fly. It doesn't explode. It clatters uselessly into the back of one of the big trucks.

Well, shit.

Athena's got no idea what the effective minimum distance is for the shells. She guesses the warhead didn't have time to charge. Or it was a dud. Who fuckin knows.

She slings the M79. Pulls her 1911. Puts bullets in the two nearest Wraiths.

Three others charge her.

She drops one with a .45 round to the face. Jukes left as his body topples to the right. She ducks a wild knife swing from the next. Slams the butt of her pistol into the side of the Wraith's head. Knees him hard in the upper thigh and shoves his raggedy ass hard enough to send him flailing off the train.

Athena frees the sawed-off with her left hand. Fires once toward another Wraith. The pellet spread is enough to tear into the fucker she'd aimed at as well as cripple another rushing in behind him.

Some kid with a machine gun near the front of the train goes Rambo. She can see the flashes from the mounted gun in the dome.

Wraiths jitter as rounds find em. Their bodies jerk. A spastic dance. Three fall in quick succession. Others in the boarding parties drop to hug the metal roof.

Which's fuckin great and all, except Athena's downrange of those bullets too.

One burrows through her leather jacket near the waist.

Another pierces her high in the right shoulder.

A third carves a trough through her left forearm.

Athena hits the deck. Growls. In pain and frustration. She screams in the dark morning air. "I'm on your side you stupid fucks."

She holsters her guns. Crawls forward. Under the barrage of bullets. Leaves a trail of blood on the roof that's black in the light.

The machine gun fire halts. Dumb kid probably outta ammo. Gotta reload.

Surviving Wraiths see their chance. Five rally. Surge toward the domed gun placement.

Athena's less inclined to help the trigger-happy motherfucker.

She keeps crawling. Moves on her knees and elbows. Her left hand shakes. Her right shoulder splashes blood against the Bulldozer's metal.

Someone grabs one of her feet. Tries to drag her back.

A Wraith she didn't quite kill. He's got both hands locked around her left ankle.

Athena kicks her heel into his face. Once. Twice. Breaks his mask. Her boot shoves the shattered pieces into his face. They flay his flesh.

He gives up when both eyes are gone.

She pulls herself toward the gunner's hole in the roof. Wants to enter with some grace but tumbles right the hell through and lands with a dull thud atop some supply crates inside the freight car.

Athena groans. Rolls off the crates. Stands. Feels her hands grow increasingly sticky from the blood that coats em. She winces. Her shoulder protests as she unholsters her 1911. Drops the mag that's in it. Loads a fresh one.

She tries to hold it up. To aim her piece.

But her right arm trembles with the effort. Won't be easy to get a good shot off.

She returns the 1911 to its home on her thigh. Opts for the shotgun since she sure as shit won't have to aim as well.

Screams nearby.

Gunfire.

Clangs of metal weapons.

A girl crying. Her voice suddenly silenced and followed by a wet gurgle.

That sorrowful voice replaced by a boy's.

Athena staggers on. Blinks. Shakes her head against the blood loss.

The kids ain't guarding the doors anymore. They're all open. She lets herself through.

There's a boy cradling the body of a young girl in his arms in the next freight car. He weeps. Doesn't go for his gun when Athena enters. He's fixated on the female corpse—she's got a massive red hole in her chest.

The bodies of two Wraiths lay nearby. Both riddled with bullets.

At least the boy ain't completely worthless.

Athena stumbles onward. Marches toward the sounds of combat.

Violence.

The train shudders. The lights flicker. Go out.

Athena pauses at the next door. Peers through the window. Sees nothing but darkness on the other side.

She takes a breath. Hefts the sawed-off.

Senses movement.

Two yellow eyes appear in the window. They hover there. Bob with the motion of the Bulldozer.

Athena stares back. Sneers.

The yellow eyes retreat. Disappear somewhere in the darkness of the freight car.

She grunts. Pushes through into the black. The door slides shut.

There's a faint light at the far end of the car. Emergency lighting that bleeds through from the passenger cabins.

Athena takes an unsteady step. Heavy boots thud. She pans the shotgun back and forth in front of her. Listens for some sign of the Wraith bastards.

Hard to tell with all the damn noise. The chugging of the train. The chains and restraints and the boxes of supplies in the freight car that shift and clang together as the Bulldozer rocks on the tracks.

She goes slow. Only a couple steps at a time.

Then Athena hears it.

Ragged breaths through a respirator.

Right behind her.

Athena doesn't turn. She flips the shotgun over her shoulder. Fires

A liquid pitter patter follows the thunderous shout of the sawed-off blast.

Now she turns. Sees the dual yellow eyes on the ground.

They don't move.

Athena does.

Creeps along. Keeps that faint emergency lighting in front of her.

She ain't sure why she's moving toward the head of the train. The medical bay and its wonderful painkillers are behind her.

Just a feeling in her gut. . . .

A feeling that if things've gone this sideways on the Bulldozer, she'll find Mark with his sister in the kitchen. . . . The next car.

Athena stops. Blinks.

This'd be a great fuckin plan if she hadn't thrown down with Colette a little while ago and forced her to put her bitchpup Emma in charge of food preparation.

Athena groans. Reloads the shotgun. Figures she'll check out the kitchen anyway.

The smells of canned, processed food is pungent. Stronger even than the combined stenches of blood and gunpowder.

That's what fills her nose before her eyes can register all the bodies. Before her ears recognize the huffing and puffing of a young girl trying to catch her breath after so much murderous exertion.

Athena keeps her shotgun up. Edges into the kitchen car. Almost slips in the gallons of Chef Boyardee that cover the floor. Beefaroni noodles intermingle with the striking red sauce and the blood from fallen Wraiths.

Ten.

Ten fallen Wraiths. Their bodies broken and bloody and filled with holes and sometimes missing an appendage or two.

Athena traces the violence to its source: Emma. The girl's jumpsuit more dark crimson than khaki. She holds a Beretta 9mm pistol in her left hand. A machete in her right. Her head and hands are red. Blood drips from her.

Emma breathes heavily.

Her blue eyes stare into Athena's.

Both women watch the other. Exhaustion in their faces and lungs.

Athena juts her chin to the gore that covers Emma's clothes.

Emma takes another deep breath. Says, "Not mine."

Athena nods. Offers the Traker girl a little thumbs-up. Turns around. Continues her slow march—now toward the rear of the train.

Her vision's starting to get kinda shitty. Blurry.

She's gonna need a little morphine. Topped by some uppers. Probably a blood bag.

Athena stumbles.

Definitely a blood bag.

She squints. Passes back through the freight cars. Through the guts that've been spilled. Over the corpses of kids and Wraiths who've been slaughtered.

There's a shape up ahead. Dark. Its back is to Athena. Her vision ain't great right now, but she sees the rags. Lifts the shotgun.

Before she can pull the trigger, the shape drops.

In its place is the visage of a ferocious Mark. Scalpel in his fist. Michelle's behind him. She grips his shirt. One eye is wide over Mark's shoulder.

Athena arches her eyebrows at em.

Mark waves her forward. "Come on, come on."

Athena grunts. Plops her ass down on one of the medical bay beds. She tries to count the number of Trakers in various stages of injury in the bay with her. Can't. Could be three. Could be nine. She can't focus.

Nurses run up and down the stairs. They're stained by great splashes of blood.

Mark glances over Athena's wounds. Hisses through his teeth. "I'll have to deal with these later, but I'm guessing you aren't looking for treatment right now."

Athena shakes her head. "Just gimme blood and, like, all the drugs." She snaps her fingers. "Now now now. I gotta explode things." She wobbles where she is on the bed. Teeters a little like a top. She hears Led Zeppelin on the radio Michelle always has with her. "When the Levee Breaks."

Mark holds her wrist. Checks her pulse.

She smacks his hand away. "Don't knock me out or act like you're my private physician. I gotta *go*."

Mark cocks an eye at her. Then at his sister.

Michelle shrugs.

Mark puffs his cheeks. Says, "Well, seeing you hopped up on amphetamines should be absolutely terrifying." He cups his hands around his mouth. Shouts. "Bridgette! I need a bag of type O-negative." He points to Athena. "Take off the jacket."

She grumbles. Sheds her leather. Her thermal undershirt is torn and stained. Stained from sweat and blood. Not that she cares how she looks in front of the doc.

Mark grabs a packet of Celox blood clotting solution. Rips it open. Pours it on the Hellcat driver's shoulder. The hemostat flakes gel when they hit her blood. Mark packs more of the Celox into the bloody hole. Then he quickly wraps her shoulder in layers of gauze.

For her forearm, he pours rubbing alcohol over it. Wraps it.

The nurse hands him a blood bag.

He runs a clear plastic tube into it. Squeezes the bag so the chambers fill. Makes sure there's no air in the line. He hands Michelle the bag. She holds it up.

Mark guides the needle at the other end of the blood tube into an artery near the crook of Athena's elbow. Lays some tape on top of it. He nods to Michelle.

She rolls her eyes. "Yeah, I got it." Lifts the blood bag higher.

Mark jogs away to another area of the medical bay.

Athena slides her arms back into her leather jacket. Looks up to Michelle. "Well." She feigns a smile. "Don't I feel like the belle of the fuckin ball here."

Michelle smirks. "Can't have the most useful murderer on the train dropping dead, can we?"

"Yeah yeah yeah." Athena waves a hand.

Mark returns. Hands her two spansules. Pills Athena doesn't recognize.

She says, "Fuck're those?"

"Dexedrine. Two fifteen-milligram doses." He cocks an eye at her. "A performance-enhancing military tradition. I have no idea when you last ate or how much booze is still in your system but it won't take long to kick in."

She pops em in her mouth. Builds up enough spit to swallow em. Coughs after she does. Grunts. Stands. Pulls the strap tight on the black duffel. Grabs the blood bag from Michelle. Tosses it in with the 40mm grenade launcher shells.

Mark winces. Doesn't bother telling the Hellcat driver that that's both risky in terms of the bag being ruptured and kinda stupid.

Athena checks her shotgun. Loaded. And a handful of shells in her jacket pocket. She holsters it. Preps mags for her 1911. One in the gun and two extra in pouches at the small of her back. She makes sure the grenade launcher is ready to go.

She nods to Mark and Athena. Heads up to the roof.

More kids on the second floor. They watch ceaselessly out the windows.

Seems like when the shit hit the fan, most Traker children ran here. Or they retreated here. Backs against the wall with a doctor nearby. Not the worst plan. *Or they all got stuck here when they tried to bring the wounded in for treatment.*

Athena reaches for the roof hatch's built in ladder. Hears one of the boys below say, "More trucks? How the hell do they have so many trucks?"

She wonders the same thing. Wonders how they have so many trucks *and* so many people. She grips the ladder. Expects there to be a shitload of pain in her shoulder as she tests her weight. And there is some. But she's also starting to feel. . .pretty goddamn good.

Stronger. Faster. More alert. More focused.

She remembers, too, something David always said: *The problem with drugs is how awesome they are.*

Athena hauls herself up to the roof of the Bulldozer. A few scattered Wraiths remain. She ain't so worried about those. A few bullets for each. Either from her or the Traker kids still in the fight.

Thing that concerns her is the trucks the kid was talking about.

Where are these fuckin trucks? She doesn't see any more transports keeping pace with the train. No more big diesel beasts offloading Wraiths.

She squats on the roof. Sees em when she realizes what she's looking for.

Three sets of headlights coming from the south. Maybe four hundred feet out.

Headlights coming straight at the goddamn train.

Wraiths ain't gonna try to board and take over the Bulldozer anymore.

They're gonna ram the hell out of it. Knock it off the rails.

And that'll just totally fuck up Athena's plans.

Scattered machine gun reports crack through the air. Bullets and tracers impact against the trucks. Do no noticeable damage.

Hard to crack through all the reinforced metal. From the front and the sides, the damn things are like tanks. Small arms fire ain't gonna punch em down.

Three hundred feet.

Athena crouches. Takes aim. Lobs a 40mm shell in the first truck's direction.

The explosion tears up its front wheels. Blows up mounds of dirt and dust. Sends rubber flying. Doesn't stop the beastly truck. It surges on.

Athena fires again.

The grenade impacts on the scrap metal sheets protecting the driver. Tears em all away. Sends the corrugated plates skittering along the ground. The glass behind the sheets ruptures. A chunk of metal smashes into the driver's face. Leaves a smudge where his head had been. The engine smokes. Flames lick at the grill.

Now the truck's a non-threat. Even if there are some assholes who survived, their ride is busted to hell.

Two hundred feet.

Athena reloads.

Her next grenade lands near the right rear of another truck. Ruptures one of the fuel tanks. The secondary explosion lifts the vehicle a good five feet in the air. Throws it to the side. Another explosion splits the whole damn thing. Sends any Wraiths inside tumbling around in the dirt. They drop and roll to put out the flames that cling to their rags. Their skin.

The final truck's closing fast. Driven by a Wraith who probably doesn't wanna get thumped the way his shithead pals have.

A Wraith atop the Bulldozer runs at Athena from her left.

She snaps her aim. Fires the M79 at the bastard.

The shell doesn't explode at this close range, but it's got enough kinetic force in it to crush his ribs and puncture his lungs.

It slams into him. A 40mm hammer blow.

Bye-bye.

The final Wraith truck is inside a hundred-fifty feet. It spews black smoke. Roars forward.

Athena's grenade splashes fire across its protected windshield. Knocks scrap loose.

Doesn't stop it though.

She digs in her bag.

No more grenades.

Athena slings the M79. Scrambles for the hatch opening. Figures it's better to be inside when the truck rams her passenger car.

A different roar emerges from the dust. Deep and bassy. An animal of some kind. Big.

She ducks on the roof. Grabs hold.

The Wraith truck gets closer and closer.

Then there's a tremendous explosion from the ground. An eruption of dirt. Flesh pulses at the center of it. Pale ribs of muscle that follow the train tracks. No eyes. Just this *thing* that bursts from the surface of the ground then dives back in serpentine motions. Its arches eclipse the Bulldozer.

Another breaches on the southern side. Follows the tracks the same way.

An endless squirming titan.

A worm with a song.

A land whale.

Athena holds onto the metal below her. Around her.

The Wraith truck slams into the broad side of the northernmost land whale. The worm doesn't care. Its ribbed flesh and muscle shudder with the impact.

But the creature keeps right on diving. Breaching.

The truck crumples against its bulk. The cab collapses. The driver becomes a smear. Wraiths in the back jump and flee.

The land whale's song rings through the morning air again. Beams of orange and red light glisten in the slime that oozes between the ribbed flesh.

Athena rests her cheek on her forearm. She watches the worms around em as they breach and dive and follow the Bulldozer along its path. For miles these enormous and beautifully ugly beasts flank the train.

She grins and lights a cigarette.

14.

"The land whales follow us through most of Illinois and Iowa and sometimes Nebraska. Dad and some of the older Trakers say it's got to do with the soil that used to be good for farming." Emma shrugs. "Wraiths don't know what to do with em. Can't fight them or get through them." She's on a cot next to Athena getting minor wounds patched up and a saline drip for dehydration. Exhaustion. "I've seen them since I was a little girl. It's the closest I've ever gotten to swimming with dolphins. Or, y'know, real whales."

Athena nods. She's still jacked up on meds. Quiet while Mark digs into her shoulder to search for the 5.56 round that impacted there.

In a few hours, if not sooner, she knows she's gonna crash hard from the Dexedrine wearing off and the morphine Mark pumped into her kicking in.

Her heart feels weird. Like it's malfunctioning.

She takes a pull of whiskey. Figures: *Fuck it.*

If her heart decides to do some off-tempo mambo and give out, she's in the right place. Mark oughtta be able to get her back on her feet. . . .

Emma watches her. Says, "Word around the Bulldozer is that you're part robot. That that's the reason you're such a good fighter."

Mark stifles a laugh. Bites his lip. He looks as surprised as anyone else that a chuckle was his response to the physical trauma Athena will spend the rest of her life with thanks to Doc Frankie.

So he stops. His mouth becomes a thin line again. Brow furrows in concentration.

He digs back inside Athena's shoulder. Tweezers and forceps and fingers red.

Athena groans as she reaches for her right leather pant leg. Pulls it up. Beyond her boot. Up beyond the knee.

The metal appendage shines in the light of the medical bay. Doc Frankie's machinery by way of Mark.

She flexes the leg. Chrome with some hidden blue LEDs that glow near the seams.

Emma doesn't say anything. She stares.

Athena says, "It ain't much more than a prosthetic leg."

Emma keeps her eyes on it. "What happened?"

Athena's eyes bounce from Mark to Michelle then to Emma. "Little while ago, the three of us here got kidnapped by a real motherfucker named Doc Frankie. He made our lives miserable. We killed the shit outta him and moved on."

Emma's eyes snap up to the Hellcat driver's. "We heard about that."

Athena blinks. Slow. The morphine's fighting the Dexedrine in her.

Emma says, "And why are you trying to get to California?"

"Why do you give a shit."

Emma glances around the medical bay. Shrugs. "I might be able to help."

"We're already doing what we gotta to make your folks happy. We can drive from Denver."

Emma sucks her teeth. "There's a good chance the Trakers aren't gonna let you go." She looks to Mark. "Why would they want to lose a doctor?" She looks to Michelle. "Why would they want to lose a baby and a potential bride?"

Athena squints. "I'll kill em if it comes to that."

"Oh, they know you will. I'm sure that's why they asked me to have a 'friendly fire incident' during the last Wraith attack."

"Now I'm gonna kill em anyway."

"And that's what *I'm* banking on."

* * *

They reconvene in the freight car that holds the Hellcat a few hours later. Once Athena's mostly back to her usual brand of anger.

Emma gives the teenage guards there a nod.

They walk off.

Athena unlocks her car. Struts to the Hellcat's trunk. Pops it. Dumps the black duffel and the M79 inside. Always possible that she'll find more 40mm shells later on down the road. No reason to ditch the weapon.

She also takes the opportunity to restock on 12-gauge rounds and .45 ammo. Pops the slugs into their homes in her magazines. "Strangely, I made the decision a little while ago to *not* help you pups stage a *coup*." She glowers at Emma. "How fuckin certain are you that the Trakers are gonna try to take what's mine?" She slams the trunk closed.

Emma admires the Hellcat's shape. Taps the metal shutter over the front windshield.

Athena puts up a hand. "Hey." She shakes her head. Snaps her fingers. "Don't touch the car."

Emma backs off. As though she was about to prod a hot stove. "Uh. . .very certain." She crosses her arms over her chest. "Colette and Father Bill. . .hell, all the Trakers preach this religious thing, but you must've noticed that 'do no harm' isn't a part of that. If it suits their needs, they will. . .pillage."

"And this ain't just some weird murderous teenage rebellion streak? My life is a *lot* easier if there's one less group of people I need to declare war on." Athena cocks her head. "And for what it's worth, I seem to be at war with quite a few folks already."

Michelle snorts. Opens the Hellcat's passenger side door. Manages to rest her rump on it. She fiddles with the radio. Frowns. Can't get the Dapper brothers anymore. Just static.

She sighs and gives up. Rests the radio on the floor.

Mark clears his throat. "Okay, let's take a step back here. Define 'pillage' for us, huh?"

"All right." Emma sniffs. "What did they tell you about all the young people who are here? That they're the children of Trakers? That this is a rite of passage and that's why there are no older fighters?"

Mark shifts his weight from one foot to the other. "More or less, yeah."

"Well, it's more or less bullshit."

Athena lights a cigarette. Blows smoke. "Colette and Father Bill ain't your parents?"

"No. They are. But as far as I can tell, I'm the only one. The other kids were all stolen. Torn away from other groups who got in the Trakers' way. Now, don't get the wrong idea. For what it's worth, the Trakers do take the kids in. Train them. But that's only so they can swell their own ranks. And all this equipment we've got? Same deal."

Mark chances a glance at Athena.

She shrugs. Motions for him to go ahead.

He says, "Well, no offense, but how is this a bad thing?"

Emma huffs. Rolls her eyes. A very typical teenage maneuver.

Jesus, why don't you understand?

Though Michelle's played that same look plenty.

Emma says, "It's wrong. They're pretending to be the good guys, but they're killing and stealing and they aren't doing any of it to better anyone but themselves."

Athena licks her lips. "Kid, you'da had a blast before the germ hit."

Michelle laughs. "If you're so pissed off that the Trakers are just opportunists, then why were you such a massive bitch to me? Why do you give a fuck about who I was with when I got pregnant."

Athena nods. "Definitely beating that fundamentalist drum."

Emma's fists tighten at her sides. "I *have* to pretend to be the good Christian soldier. Colette and Father Bill scrutinize me more than anyone else."

"So *that* was a ploy, but *this* is legit."

"Right."

"Ehhh. . . ." Athena holds her hand out and seesaws it back and forth. "Seems a bit thin to me."

Mark agrees. "Yeah, I'm not sure what the impetus is exactly. None of us here particularly like being used. Or conned."

Emma taps her foot. Frowns at the floor. "More of the rails are active than anyone knows. I can show you maps where the nurseries run." She looks up to her audience. "Those are the trains that raid for children. If that's not enough—" she frowns at the floor again. "I can show you an inventory list of what we've stolen. The goods that don't include kids." She cocks an eye at Michelle. "But if we are talking kids, they'll snatch your baby away too."

"What do you get out of this? You just said Colette and Bill *were* your parents. But now you're advocating, uh—" Mark looks over to Athena. "You're talking about siccing our own leather-clad sociopath on them."

Athena grins. That's a fucked up compliment, but she'll take it.

Emma furrows her brow. Her eyes water. "There was a boy. . . ." She points to Mark. "He was one of the ones you couldn't save." Emma's eyes go wide and she locks em onto Athena's. "And you saw me with that dead boy's hand in my own." She snaps her fingers. "I know you saw us and I know you know what I'm talking about."

Athena blinks. Most days are a blur at best. But she does remember that, since she was scoping out the bitchpup for weirdness.

She nods. "I saw you holding hands with a corpse, yeah. Almost soon as we got here."

Emma takes a step forward in anger. Stops. Raises a hand to her face. Turns it into a fist before her lips. Breathes. Is about to plant her open palms against the hood of the Hellcat but thinks better of it in the final moment. She groans and balls her fists again.

Emma says, "That was Caleb." Emma's voice catches in her throat. "Caleb and I were attached at the hip when we were smaller. Once we, uh—" Emma laughs. "Once we knew we were people?

Not quite adults but close. Once we knew that, you couldn't separate us. And it was. . .it was nice."

She offers a little smile to Mark. Michelle. Athena. "We loved each other. We talked a lot and we realized that things shouldn't be the way they are. It wasn't some idle idealism, either. We were sick of watching kids our age die because the Trakers don't want to put their own lives on the line. We got some of the others together and we thought, soon, that we could take over."

Emma furrows her brow. "And then, I don't know exactly what happened. Colette and Father Bill found out. Maybe they connected the dots or maybe some rotten fuck ratted on us." She shrugs. "They couldn't have me killed—I *am* their daughter, and that would look bad—but they asked Caleb to move ammo up to the turrets in the middle of the Wraith attack outside Indianapolis. For no good reason. They effectively murdered him. And I'm sure it was to shut me up and stop me." Emma's eyes water. She wipes at em. Sniffs.

Athena rubs her face. "You idiots steal babies from the Wraiths? Is that why they're up our asses?" She stares at the freight car ceiling. Stares at Emma. Sighs. Pops the Hellcat trunk. Grabs a bottle of whiskey. "If you fuck me over, you're dead." Tosses it to the Traker daughter.

Emma catches the container of amber liquid. "No the Wraiths really are just evil fuckers. No pity for them." She nods. Juts her chin at Athena. "I knew when I saw you. . . ." She takes a pull. Caps it. Tosses it back.

"You're a teenager. You don't know shit." Athena smokes. Sucks a mouthful of booze. "I'm doing this to protect what's mine. Don't get the wrong idea."

Emma nods again.

Michelle says, "This is adorable, but is there a plan? And how can I avoid being a part of it." She points to her giant belly. "This is not the body of someone who's combat-ready."

Athena and Mark look to Emma.

Emma scratches her cheek. Squints. Thinks.

Mark says, "Well. . .I've been on my feet more or less since we left Indianapolis and working my ass off. Everyone's seen that. Dexedrine is keeping me upright. If Michelle hides in the Hellcat, I can too under the guise that I'm taking a break. I don't think that would make anyone suspicious."

Emma's eyes remain locked on the metal floor. "Yeah. That'll work. There are one or two people that I trust that I can post back here as well. I'm going to need the rest of them up with me if we're doing this, though."

Athena drops her cigarette. Grinds it out. "If this's gonna be some kinda red team-blue team deal, how'm I supposed to know who not to kill?"

"My people will know not to engage you." She pauses. "We'll all have black tactical gloves on. That should stand out but not enough to get us caught before it goes down. The others. . .they *will* try to kill you."

Athena mulls it over. Points to Emma. "When this is over, you get us to Denver and we go our separate ways. No backstabbing bullshit."

"Of course not." Emma shakes her head. "That's the whole reason we're doing this. I actually *do* believe in a righteous cause."

"Yeah. All right." Athena cracks her neck. Digs a hand into her jacket pocket. Produces the key fob for the Hellcat. Bounces it in her hand. She looks to Mark. "I'm trusting you with this." She throws the key fob to him.

Mark catches. Nods his head.

Athena loads the two spare shotguns the Dapper brothers gave em. Hands one to Mark. Hands the other to Michelle. "Point and click. Don't let anyone near the car."

She gestures to Emma. "Let's go."

15.

Far as Athena can tell, nothing's different. It's still Traker kids who look like they don't know their asses from their elbows. Only now some of em have black gloves on.

She reminds herself not to shoot those teens as she walks through to the train in the direction of the engine.

There still ain't any actual "plan" to speak of. Athena's really just waiting for Emma or one of her people to open fire. Then carry on through that. Kill everything that moves. Kill Colette and Father Bill especially. Wait to see if those rebellious kids turn on her. Kill *them* if that's the case.

Could make outta this deal with a train and its cargo to play with.

That wouldn't be bad.

There's still the issue of Colette supposedly asking Emma to kill her during the Wraith attack. Which didn't happen. So when's that nun bitch gonna do something about it or raise hell?

Shaky. This whole thing is shaky.

Athena grunts. Looks out one of the north-facing windows.

Land whales surge through the ground all around. The worms cry out. Their song manages to overtake the usual hustle and bustle on the train. Manages to overwhelm the vibrations and the engine.

She wonders if they think the train is one of them. Their pack leader come to guide them toward Colorado. The vibrations must be similar. Or *feel* similar to the big bugs. And the Bulldozer horn, as it goes off at irregular intervals, could be a sort of song to the insects.

Athena sees Emma in between the first car and the engine. She stands on the coupler. The girl's got her black gloves on. Got a compact bullpup submachine gun in her hands. A P90 with its funky design where the mag loads on top. It's less than a foot long.

Emma says, "I can get into the engine from here. I'll do it quiet and knock both Colette and Father Bill out. You go up top. Wait for me. I'll open the side door. There aren't any Trakers manning the guns so you don't have to worry about that. If we can take the engine then we can just work backward through the train."

Athena sniffs.

Thinks: *I'm taking orders from a disgruntled teen.*

Says, "You can drive the Bulldozer?"

"I am my father's daughter." She smirks. "Go."

Athena grips the ladder on the side of the coupling. Hauls herself up. Nods to Emma and jumps across to the engine car's roof.

She crouches. Takes it slow while the wind whips at her. Also doesn't wanna stomp too loud and give herself away.

Even though this shit's all gonna go wrong anyway.

She eyes the land whales. Big and dumb and simple.

And she envies em.

Athena makes her way above the door. Gets on her belly. Watches for the scrap to come undone so she can get inside.

And waits.

And waits.

She takes a deep breath. Exhales through her nose. Leans farther over the side to see.

Any time now, Emma. Any goddamn time.

The door unlocks. Opens inward.

The scrap metal shudders outward. Explodes in a storm of debris. Pieces fly and bounce off the body of the big land whale tracking the train.

At the center of the maelstrom is Emma. Her arms flailing.

She collides with the side of the worm. Thuds to the ground in a puff of dust.

Athena sneers. Looks down.

Colette's got a pistol aimed at her fuckin head. A big revolver.

Athena jerks backward on the roof as the nun pulls the trigger. She scrambles. Bullets punch up through the engine car roof. Athena kicks her legs. Rolls. Gets to her feet. Stomps farther back in a hurry. Jumps back over to the first passenger car.

Getting inside seems like a smart idea.

She runs to the first mounted gun. Climbs inside the scrap dome.

Some young Traker's trying to climb up.

No gloves.

Athena kicks down. Smashes the kid's fingers. Her heel smacks into the bridge of the boy's nose. Cracks it. Blood flows in small rivers.

She kicks again and again.

The kid falls down into the passenger car. She jumps after. Lands on him. Her boots crush his chest. Red bursts from his mouth in a thick bubble. Paints Athena's leather pants with his hemoglobin.

Some other asshole shouts at her. A chick with an assault rifle.

Athena pulls her sawed-off. Buckshot tears away the girl's face. Pellets peel away skin and muscle. They break the bitch's teeth too.

The Hellcat driver breaks open the shotgun. Clears the spent shell. Replaces it with a fresh one. Holsters the sawed-off. Plucks up the trimmed down M4 assault rifle this dumb dead Traker teenager wasn't fast enough with.

Another Traker emerges at the stairwell. Black gloves on the hands of a young brunette. The brunette a little bloody, but combat effective. Her finger rests on the trigger guard of an AK-47. She makes sure not to point it at Athena.

Athena keeps the red dot trained on the girl anyway. Says, "Downstairs?"

"This car is clear. Where's Emma?"

"Outside somewhere."

The brunette frowns. "All right. I need to keep moving back through the cars to meet up with the others and get rid of those shithead loyalists. Can you take the engine?"

"Yeah. How many of you are there?"

The brunette cocks an eye. "You mean how many of us are left? To be honest, I have no idea."

Gunshots sound off somewhere in the train. The light cracks of an automatic. And the heavy chugs of a larger caliber weapon.

Someone's putting up a fight.

The brunette rebel heads toward the commotion.

Athena grunts. Not really sure she's up to the task of turning this whole dumb thing around. She lights a cigarette. Takes a moment.

The car she's in is perfectly quiet. Only noises are the engine. The gentle dripping and settling of the dead.

Dawns on Athena that other than killing the fuckin nun and the priest, she doesn't have a damn clue what she's doing. She can't drive a train.

She blows smoke through her nose. Bites her lip.

Mutters. "Fuck it."

She marches down the stairs. Walks out onto the coupler. Pounds on the door to the engine.

Colette's face appears in the door window. Her brow furrowed. She smiles at Athena. Shakes her head. Slow.

Athena just points. Presses her index finger against the glass. Cocks her thumb back as a hammer. Pulls the figurative trigger.

She goes back up the ladder. Jumps onto the engine roof. Realizes in that instant that she doesn't have a fuckin clue how to get inside.

The Bulldozer shakes. It veers off the more or less straight shot it's been on. Makes a hard left. Seems to be headed in a new direction. South.

Athena wonders exactly what just happened and if it was supposed to.

There's a huge sprawling scrapyard on the right. Cargo containers stacked thirty or forty feet high in some spots. Figures mill around on top of em. Opposite the scrapyard are watchtowers with even more figures.

Athena deduces that this ain't good.

She scrambles to get back inside. The roof feels kinda. . .like she's gonna get shot to shit if she stays exposed. She lands on the kid's corpse again when she jumps in. She leaves bloody boot prints behind her as she jogs to rejoin the fight.

No big wait there.

The rebel girl she saw before is locked in a wrestling match with a loyalist boy. The two roll around in the blood and viscera of their comrades.

Athena doesn't bother trying to line up a shot with the M4. She stomps toward the tussle. Uses her rifle butt to clock the loyalist in the back of the head.

He falls over. Out cold.

Athena puts a bullet in his face. Doesn't want the little puke waking up later to make her life difficult. She offers her hand to the rebel girl.

Rebel girl takes it. Huffs as she gets to her feet.

The two exchange no words. They charge on. Link up with two rebel boys. Another girl. Another boy.

The rebel group slaughters their way to the Hellcat.

They find Mark and a rebel girl near the door. Blood on both. Not their own. Spent shell casings on the floor. Two dead loyalists. One dead rebel boy. Michelle still in the Hellcat.

When Athena opens the passenger door, the pregnant woman's got her shotgun in Athena's face.

The Hellcat driver grabs the barrel. Pushes it away. "That'd be a shitty way to end things." She snatches the scattergun.

Michelle gasps. "I just peed a little." She rubs her belly. "I didn't know kids were such fuckers." She talks to her uterus. "Don't be like them, okay?"

Athena smirks at the display. Catches herself.

Static crackles over an unseen speaker.

Athena whirls on the rebel kids. "You guys have a fuckin radio networked throughout the train? And nobody ever uses it?"

The kids eye her. Don't say anything.

Michelle pipes up. "To be fair, everyone else knew they had working radios. You were just. . .drunk most of the time."

Athena blinks. Tilts her head. Can't argue against that.

Colette's voice slithers from the speakers. "This is for all you. . .heathens out there. You festering heretics and the Hellcat bitch who *turned my own daughter against me.* We've pulled south of what used to be called Pacific Junction. Just shy of Nebraska. This is one of our strongholds. Welcome to Big Scrap. I look forward to not ever seeing any of you again."

Mark's eyes go wide. He pans his gaze to Athena.

Athena stifles a laugh. Blows her cheeks out. "All right." She puts her hands on her hips. "Guess Colette's feeling super-villainy." She looks to the rebel kids. "We gotta lock this car down tight. Nothing gets in or out."

The front-facing door on the freight car flies open.

Emma steps in. Blood clumps in the dust on her clothes.

She says, "We got problems."

16.

Emma says, "Colette knew something was up."

Athena says, "She's a nun. I'm Polish. Raised Catholic. Lemme tell you, nuns are spooky motherfuckers. Telepaths in terms of sins you didn't know you were committing."

"Yeah." Emma tosses down a fat duffel bag. It clangs on the metal floor. She snaps her fingers at it. "That's got 40mm grenades, 5.56 STANAG mags, 12-gauge rounds and some assorted other munitions." She's still breathing heavy. "Why didn't anyone hit the barracks for ammo on the way back here?"

Athena grins. Likes this chick.

The brunette rebel girl digs into the duffel. Starts to dole out ammo. "We thought you were gone." She slides a case of 40mm grenades toward Athena. "We thought you were dead."

Emma checks the mag on her P90. Adjusts the sling on her bolt action rifle. "Momma tossed me from the train. Sure as hell didn't mean I couldn't get back on." She looks to Athena. "Hellcat?"

"What?" Athena's got the M79 again. Stuffs a fresh shell in the chamber. Smokes. Stuffs more explosives into the duffel on her back. Tosses her whiskey to Emma. "You and me? Get to killing.

Everyone else useful defends this car." Athena points around the room. "You jerks are now personally responsible for everything I care about."

The young rebels looks to Mark and Michelle.

Athena shakes her head. "I'm talking about my fuckin Hellcat."

An air raid siren shrieks. The Traker camp alarm.

Athena throws open the freight car's sliding door. Grenade launcher in hand.

A Traker outside jerks his hand back. Eyes wide. Bearded face grey. Apparently he was just about to open the door himself.

She aims without thinking. Pulls the trigger on the thumper.

The Traker's too close for the shell to arm and explode.

It hits at an angle. Punches the fucker's lower jaw off in a spray of red. His tongue wags in the dusty air. Drips. His body spasms from small bloody eruptions along his chest. Automatic weapons fire from rebels inside the freight car hammers him.

Athena reloads the grenade launcher. Slings it. Shoulders the M4 she pulled from the loyalist carcass. Peers through the red dot sight. Trains it on a Traker in one of the watchtowers. Sends five rounds his way. Three splinter the wood railing he stands behind. The last two bury themselves in his gut.

Gunshots pop the dirt near the open freight car. A round *pangs* off Athena's right robotic leg. Makes an ugly hole in her leather trousers. Another glances at her right bicep. Stings like a motherfuck but it ain't too bad.

Emma stands next to Athena. Uses her P90 to spray 5.7mm bullets at Trakers coming around the rear of the train. She takes out a few knees. Blows more holes in their chests and heads when they hit the ground.

She unslings her bolt action rifle. Takes a knee. Rests her cheek on the stock. Brings the barrel to bear on the other Trakers in the watchtowers. She takes three shots. Three bodies crumple.

That's all for the possible snipers.

Eastern side of the Bulldozer should be clear.

Athena drops to the ground. Peers under the train car for boots on the other side. Sees a few pairs. She pulls her 1911. Fires into enemy feet. Seven tight splashes of blood.

She pops out her empty mag. Slams a new one in.

When the Trakers hit the ground from their wounds, she puts .45 slugs in their faces.

Four fewer assholes to worry about.

Now it's a matter of clearing out that camp. Big Scrap.

No way to know how many Trakers are still there.

Place's layout is a mystery too.

She and Emma work their way around to the back of the final freight car. Poke their heads out to get a read on the situation.

There's those big damn walls made outta cargo containers. Maybe ten guys staring down from on top.

Good news is those walls are less than a hundred feet away. Not *too much* ground to sprint across.

Bad news is there's fuckall for cover.

Emma holds up a finger. *Wait.*

She charges to the left down the length of the Bulldozer on the safer side.

Athena watches her climb up one of the passenger cars. Position herself low enough to maintain cover but also use the roof to steady her rifle. The girl aims slow. Deliberate.

Fires.

Drops a Traker from the wall.

The other gunners turn to focus on Emma's position, but the chick's already hopped down. She's moving to another sniper hide farther down the line.

Athena takes the opportunity to emerge.

Fires a wild shot with the M79. Doesn't really give a shit where along the wall the grenade lands. Just wants to make some unexpected noise.

The grenade goes boom about two hundred feet away. Punches in the side of a fat cargo container. The damage is negligible, but the impact on the demeanor of the Trakers is grand.

One shouts. "Jesus Christ, they've got explosives too."

Another shouts. "This is the Hellcat? And Father Bill's kid?"

"Yeah."

"Fuck."

"Just get the goddamn bruisers out there."

Athena grunts. Dumps the spent shell casing. Reloads. Waits for the *crack* of Emma's rifle. Hears it. Pops out again. Aims this time. Right at one of the upper containers that's got an occupant.

The 40mm boom boom turns some dumb Traker up there into an eruption of red. A skin-colored sack of gore torn open and raining down.

Athena chuckles.

The doors on one of the cargo containers open.

Three figures step out. All in massive bomb disposal suits. All toting black Mk48 machine guns with fat box magazines attached to the bottom.

The bastards are slow. Bulletproof, but really. . .really slow. Scary in their faceless, plodding malicious intent. . . . But still really fuckin *slow*.

Athena sniffs. Sends a grenade into the cluster of em.

The 40mm shell explodes just behind em. Inside the metal cargo container. It knocks all three forward. One trips. Lands on his face. A sumo wrestler overburdened by Kevlar and equipment.

She sends another boom boom at em. It erupts in the dirt. Tears one of the bruiser's feet off. Concusses the one on the ground so he ain't moving anymore. Maybe his insides are liquid now from the blast wave.

Doesn't matter.

A third grenade sails by the group. Explodes against the wall. Makes the heavy cargo containers shake.

A fourth grenade makes em teeter. Fall.

In cartoonish fashion, the metal shipping containers tumble. Almost slow motion.

The two bruisers who're still active throw their hands up.

Metal smashes em. Crushes em.

And the bruisers are no more.

Truth be told, the bruisers were a dumb idea.

Now the wall to Big Scrap is open. Anyone inside is fair game.

Michelle screams. A blood-curdling wail.

Athena rushes back to the Hellcat cargo area. Jump up inside. Surveys the scene.

Rebel kids stands in a protective semicircle around Michelle.

The pregnant brunette cradles the carcass of Mark. Her brother's face is contorted in fear. Mouth open in a silent scream. Brow furrowed. A frozen moment of terror. Awareness.

There are no wounds on his body.

But Athena's seen that look before.

She squints. Locks eyes with one of the rebel kids. "Fuck happened?"

The rebel kid—an Asian boy about thirteen—shakes his head. "He just. . .fell." His mouth is agape. "Maybe he had a heart attack I don't know."

Athena groans.

It wasn't a fuckin heart attack. She knows the face. The frozen shock.

That's how all the germ victims looked.

Which she doesn't understand. At all.

Thoughts fly through her head. Snippets of shit she's overheard.

Mason on and on about how "West *is* death and dust for folks from the east."

Father Bill jawing. Talking about how all the background radiation might've been a weird kinda cure for the cancer and the germ, but if you were still carrying the germ. . .say from the east. . . .

Athena knows there's no point in trying to console Michelle. The pregnant woman still shrieking. Her arms wrapped around her brother.

So she doesn't bother.

The Bulldozer jerks underfoot.

Athena whirls around to the door. The landscape starts to move by.

They're on their way south again.

Emma jumps into the freight car. Frowns at Michelle and Mark's body. Eyes Athena. "I think they're gonna drag us through more Traker outposts on the way to Houston."

The Hellcat driver walks in a deliberate slow pace toward the brother and sister. Doesn't shove her hands into Mark's pockets, but gingerly, respectfully, plucks the Dodge keys from his flannel breast pocket.

Michelle looks to her. Face red. Tears cut wet paths through the grime on the pregnant woman's cheeks.

Athena takes a deep breath. Nods once. Stands. Points at the rebel kids. Says, "Get the Hellcat unhitched and kick open the rear loading door."

17.

The Hellcat purrs.

Big engine idles.

Athena holds the brakes. Shifts it into neutral. Taps the gas so the engine growls.

Emma is stoic in the passenger seat. Her fingers play over the M79. She breaks it open. Checks the 40mm shell inside the breach.

The rebel kids lock metal guides into place at the back of the freight car. They hang down. Bounce against the gravel along the tracks.

Athena releases the brakes.

The Hellcat rolls backward. Fast. Down the guides, then they're in the dirt.

She floors it. Matches speed with the Bulldozer. Starts to pull ahead past the freight car with the rebels. Notices in the rearview that survivors from Big Scrap have brought out their own toys to play.

Off-roads and pickup trucks. Fords and Chevys. Some quad bikes. Shit that's meant to maintain speed across the dusty farmlands.

They're catching up. Fast.

Hellcat wasn't really built to outrun vehicles in the dirt.

Emma rolls her window down. Sits on the door frame. Half outta the Dodge. She shoulders the grenade launcher. Fires.

An explosion tears through the first of the pursuing trucks. Its hood shoots up. The engine burns. It skids sideways. Rolls onto its side. Ends up on its roof.

Someone tries to crawl out.

The gas tank blows. Flambés the escapee.

A quad bike revs up on Athena's left.

She slows so it can catch up.

Balances her sawed-off on the door.

She fires both barrels. The shotgun bucks hard. Pellets cloud the air. Tear into the quad driver. He slumps off. His vehicle rumbles forward and comes to an undramatic stop.

Rebel kids in the open freight car lay their own fire on the Trakers. They take out the rest of the quads. The drivers too exposed to withstand the onslaught of lead.

The windshield on another truck becomes a spider web. The man at the wheel half-blind and then his forehead shatters when a rebel bullet punches into it.

Athena cranks up the horsepower.

One truck still in the hunt. A big old Ford F250. This one with a machine gunner in the flatbed. He shoots into the freight car. An M249 burping out a high volume of 5.56 rounds.

The rebel kids don't have any option except to take cover.

They seal the freight car back up. Shut the doors.

Emma takes aim again with the M79. Fires.

The shell falls short. Blows up nothing but a patch of dead land.

Bullets fly forward from the truck. Bursts of gunfire. Fresh holes appear along the Hellcat's trunk. They smash the glass and bang against the metal shutter in the back.

All while the pickup closes the distance between itself and the Dodge.

Athena jukes the Hellcat. Jitters it left and right. Not enough to cause a spinout. Just enough to hopefully screw with the gunner's aim.

Emma reloads.

Athena's not sure there's enough room for the grenade to arm itself. Waits to see what'll happen.

The shell soars. Clangs off the front windshield. Leaves a crack there instead of a glorious, machine-eating explosion.

Well, fuck.

A bullet tears through Emma's right hand. Takes off the girl's pinky and ring fingers. Another grazes her left side. Just above the hip.

She howls. Falls back inside the Hellcat. Reaches for a random rag on the ground. Wraps her right hand in a hurry. Presses that quickly-soaked cloth against the bleeding trough in her side.

Athena breathes through her nose. Corners of her mouth pulled down in a frown.

The pickup surges forward. Its bumper kisses the Hellcat.

Athena shouts to Emma, "Drive." She keeps her foot on the gas. Pulls her 1911. Fires backward into the off-road. Tags the glass. Manages to land a .45 slug in the shoulder of the gunner.

Two hits in seven rounds ain't great but she'll take it.

She reloads. Last mag. Grabs the bag of M79 shells from the girl. Slings it over her shoulder. Works her ass onto the driver's side door frame as Emma slides over and grips the wheel with bloody hands.

Giving up control of the Hellcat pisses Athena off. But she hates these khaki-clad Traker motherfuckers more.

She scrambles onto the Dodge's roof. Stands. Hurls herself at the hood of the pickup. Clambers into the flatbed with the machine gunner. Punches. He blocks. She snaps her right robotic foot up into his balls. He shrieks. She grabs the back of his head. Smashes it against the cab exterior till his face breaks and bleeds and he ain't a problem.

The Ford driver swerves the truck.

Athena loses her footing. Crashes hard against the flatbed. Gets the wind knocked outta her. Her lips take the brunt of the damage. They split along an ugly seam and leak blood into her mouth.

She spits.

The truck driver keeps juking his vehicle like an asshole.

Athena grabs the gunner's M249. Lies on her back. Points the barrel where the driver's head should be. Holds the trigger down and sprays 5.56 rounds till they plow through the metal and the glass and the truck starts to slow.

She climbs onto the cab roof. Uses the machine gun like a bludgeon to smash the passenger side window. Slides inside.

Not much left of the driver's head. A wobbly, drippy mass of red and bone.

Athena reaches across his dead lap. Opens the door. Kicks his carcass out.

Windshield's in bad shape too. Hard to see through. All spider webs. She pushes the glass out. Clears her view.

Hits the gas.

The Ford rumbles forward. Kicks up dirt.

She catches back up to the Bulldozer.

To the Hellcat.

She looks over at Emma.

The girl's pale. Struggling to keep the car on task. She manages a nod.

Athena nods back and floors it. Pulls ahead. Pulls alongside the engine car. She grabs the big M249 and sticks it down against the gas pedal so it won't come loose.

She moves fast. Before the Ford can veer too far off course. Athena gets back on the cab roof. Jumps. She catches a railing near the back of the engine. Her boots drag against the ground for a moment but she finds her footing. Gets herself up.

Onto the coupling she goes.

Colette's at the engine door again. In the window.

The mad nun stares out at Athena. Same smile. Same slow head shake.

This time the Hellcat driver grins back. Produces a 40mm high explosive from the satchel. Holds it up. Tucks it against the base of the engine's sturdy metal door.

Colette's smile evaporates.

Athena jogs into the passenger car. Gives herself twenty feet. Turns. Aims the 1911.

Fires.

Boom.

The HE shell rocks the engine door off its hinges. Turns it into a twisted mess of metal and machinery.

Athena rushes in. Pistol in hand.

Colette's waiting for her. "I *knew* it was a mistake to let you stay here." She swings a bat at the Hellcat driver's head. "You've ruined *everything*. You harlot. You *whore*."

Athena jerks her head back. The bat misses her face. Hits the 1911 instead.

The gun skitters to the floor.

Athena puts her wrists up. Deflects another blow from Colette. Drives her knee up. Right into the nun's guts.

Colette drops to her knees. Parries a punch from Athena. Pulls the Hellcat driver down. Gets her in a lock on the ground. She pins Athena. Pinches the driver's legs together to keep her from kicking anymore.

Athena punches up. Into Colette's face. One. Two blows.

Colette locks her forearms around the square of her jaw so Athena doesn't have much to hit.

Athena knows she's pinned. So she shakes. Wriggles like a mad worm. Bucks.

Colette won't relent.

Athena grabs the nun by her ears. Pulls the bitch close. So her blues are locked onto Colette's. Says nothing but slams her forehead into the religious woman's nose. Again and again and again.

Till Colette falls backward.

Till the nun struggles with the blood spigot that used to be her nasal cavity.

Athena stands on shaky legs.

Draws her shotgun. Keeps it pointed in the general vicinity of Colette.

She marches farther into the engine. Through the tight corridor that houses the diesel turbines. Into the cab. Where Father Bill waits.

And. . . .

Man.

It's just a corpse.

A goddamn corpse.

Father Bill's body there on the controls. A puppet. A marionette. The whole fuckin thing held up by twine that Athena pokes with idle fingers.

She pants. Fights to catch her breath.

There are tape recorders nearby. Cassettes. They're labeled with different prayers. Different times. Different blessings.

Athena keeps the sawed-off pointed at Colette. "When did he die?"

Colette drags herself into the cab. Teeth stained red. "We. . .he. . . ." She groans. Spits. Coughs. "Outside Indianapolis. Before we got into Chicago Union Station. When the Wraiths. . . The Wraiths. . . ."

The Hellcat driver fingers the tapes labeled with Father Bill's prayers. "So you just ran this shit to keep everyone thinking there was a plan? That Father Bill was gonna see all those kids through the nightmare?"

Colette works herself into a sitting position. Smiles at Athena. "Father Bill's death could have been—" She catches herself. "Well, Father Bill's death could *be* the catalyst for a new movement. One that unites all of—"

Athena empties both barrels into Colette's head. Shuts the nun up.

She waggles her fingers in the air. Finds the throttle on the console. Kills the power. Slows the Bulldozer. Finds the brakes. Applies em. The train comes to a stop.

Athena looks to the mess that was Colette's face.

Grunts as she hauls the bodies of the nun and the priest outside by their collars. Really nothing left above Colette's neck.

Athena drops the corpses in the dust.

Her Hellcat glides to a halt. The pale face of Emma stares from the driver's seat.

Then the girl rests her head against the steering wheel and closes her eyes.

Athena sighs.

18.

Blood and terror and dust.

That's the legacy of the Trakers.

To be more specific: Deception. Murder. Human trafficking. Stolen children. The disguise of righteousness. Of doing God's work.

Total and utter bullshit.

And they're still out there. The oilmen in Houston still have their trains out. Running crude. Running kids.

Only thing they're missing now is the Bulldozer.

Ain't no happy rule saying they can't come back for it once they realize what the hell happened on the way to Denver.

Both nurses on the train were rebels. Nice luck there.

They patch Emma up.

Athena takes care of herself with supplies from the medical bay. Wraps wounds with gauze. Pops a few aspirin. Hisses when the whiskey from her bottle drips into her split lip.

It's tempting to help herself to a bottle of Dexedrine. So she does.

She steps outta the train. Back into the afternoon light. Digs around in her leather jacket for her smokes. Finds one. Tucks it into the corner of her mouth and lights it.

Athena breathes smoke.

When she pulls the cigarette out to ash it, the filter's stained a deep red.

She notices a new pain in her chest. Deep. When she takes in a lotta air. Could be something torn. Could be a fresh, budding tumor.

Though given what happened to Mark, she doesn't have a clue.

Radiation like chemotherapy that killed the cancer that was killing him, but with the cancer gone, the germ up and ended him.

Fuck.

The young rebels stand in a circle around a funeral pyre. They hold hands. Sounds like someone's saying a hushed prayer.

Emma stands closer to the flames. Inside the circle. Both her parents' bodies slowly turning to carbon.

Ash.

Michelle sits in the dirt some short distance away. Holds vigil over her dead brother.

The woman's since closed the dead man's eyes. Moved his mouth and facial features so they're no longer locked in a visage of shock. Fear.

Athena makes her way over. Whiskey in hand. She flicks away her stogie. Taps Michelle's shoulder with the bottle.

The pregnant brunette glances at the amber liquid. Considers the booze for a moment. Finally takes it and allows herself a single, small pull from the bottle.

Emma and the rebels march in a somber group toward Michelle and Athena.

The new leader of this child soldier group regards both the pregnant woman and the Hellcat driver before she looks down at Mark. Says, "We cremate the bodies out here so the bugs don't get them. . . . If you want. . . ." She sighs. Rubs her cheeks and her red eyes.

Michelle says nothing. She caresses Mark's face. Runs her fingers through his hair. Fidgets with his shirt to make it look nice.

She leans over and plants a kiss on his forehead.

Looks up to Emma. The young rebels. Nods.

She struggles but gets to her feet all right.

Emma and the others walk to the train. They collect a few axes. Hatchets. Head a little farther out to where the dead trees stand with their grey leaves.

They chop em down. Split the logs into long lengths of wood. Stack em tight. Strong. Even make a platform for Mark's body to lay on.

The rebel kids seem to know what they're doing.

Athena lets em. Keeps her distance.

They lift Mark's body. Walk slow with it. Place it on the pyre platform.

Emma brings a burning torch from the flames of her parents. Hands it to Michelle.

The pregnant woman takes it. Her tears flow anew.

She sniffs. Watches her brother's body for a little while longer.

Then sets the pyre alight.

Athena stares at shapes farther out.

The humped over forms of land whales breaching and diving. Their cries echo across the dust.

She struts to the Hellcat. Plays her fingers along the fresh bullet holes.

19.

Emma gets the Bulldozer rolling again. Reverses it into the junction. Corrects course and gets em all moving west again.

Through Nebraska.

Which, Athena decides, is obscenely fuckin flat. Ain't nothing there except dead farmland. Dust.

Oversized spiders chase oversized grasshoppers. And oversized hornets chase em in return. Land whales sing their songs.

That's all there is.

Athena realizes it'd be easy to go nice and crazy out here.

20.

They pull into Denver that night.

The city itself completely dark under the looming Rocky Mountains. Denver Union Station is the exception. The place with its funky open air train hall. A vaguely UFO-shaped shell-roof overtop the tracks.

Directly in front of the train hall is the station terminal. It's a white stone structure. A giant central hall flanked by two shorter wing buildings with narrow windows and flower motifs.

There are signs and flags up all over. Purple with black and white text. Same color scheme as the Colorado baseball team. It reads: ROCKY RANGERS.

Athena squints in the spotlights the Bulldozer passes through. The platforms all busy with militia-looking folks and men and women in jeans. Flannels. Work boots. Heavy jackets to protect em from the cold. The weapon choices seem to consist largely of M16s and M4s as well as some hunting rifles.

These folks ain't Trakers.

That's a damn good thing.

She steps down from the open freight car and its precious Dodge cargo. Notices the attention's all on her. And her vehicle.

A tall bearded man in his late forties approaches her. He's got an armband colored the same way as the signs. He smiles. Teeth a little yellow. He holds his hand out to her. Says, "Welcome to Denver, home of the Rocky Rangers. I'm John Quincy."

Athena cocks an eye at him. Shakes and pulls away. She points down the length of the train. Toward Emma and a few of her rebels. "Think you mean to say that to her. Not me."

Quincy grins. "I know who she is, and I know who you are. Doesn't mean I don't wanna shake your hand." He gives Athena a little smirk. Then sets off to greet Emma.

Athena furrows her brow.

Thinks: *Is that guy hitting on me?*

* * *

Emma.

Emma's a clever girl.

Hated what her parents were doing under the pretenses of religion and took over. Then she negotiated a deal with the Rocky Rangers. Defected. Said the Rangers could keep the crude. Keep the cattle they were supposed to exchange for it.

But she gets to run the Bulldozer.

She and her rebels get to do things *her* way.

The right way, as far as they're concerned.

How could Quincy not be impressed by that?

He was more impressed with Athena, though.

And of course he's hitting on her.

Not quite sweet talk, but lots of suggestions she should stay. Rest for a few days. Take up residence in one of the rooms inside Union Station.

He says, "The Rangers can get you anything you want. Anything you need." His speech a fleeting mist in the cold air.

Athena checks her gear in the trunk of the Hellcat. The car parked on Wynkoop Street in front of the station terminal. She makes sure she's got spare fuel. Food. Ammo. Whiskey. Cigarettes. A few new pilfered medical items from the Bulldozer.

She says, "I don't need anything." Looks him in the eye. "Thanks, though." Thinks about what it would be like—for a heartbeat—to spend the night with this guy.

Probably pretty good.

But as soon as that thought flashes through her mind, so does the memory of David.

And she's back to being standoffish and a bit pissed.

Quincy nods. "All right. Can't blame a guy for trying." He points to his left. South. "You're gonna wanna hit Route 6. Take that to 70-West. You can cut through the Rockies that way. We've got raider activity shut down on this side of the mountains. I can't speak for the other side, though."

Athena grunts. Lights a cigarette.

Quincy watches Michelle tuck herself into the Hellcat's passenger seat and close the door without so much as a glance. He says, "What's in California, anyway?"

Athena breathes smoke. "Redwoods."

Quincy considers it. Says, "Hard to get radio from the west over all that stone, but from what we know, the New California Republic is supposed to be the folks running things out that way. No idea what they're like, but that's what we hear. Stories about those guys and their New Eden project." He shrugs. "Healthy babies."

"Right." Athena nods.

Quincy offers his hand again. Says, "See ya."

Athena takes it.

Gets into the driver's seat of her wounded Hellcat.

Rubs her chest as that new pain reminds her of its existence.

* * *

The Rockies are purple in the morning light. Purple under red and gold rays from the sun that'll be around long after the final human fills its lungs with one last gasp of air.

No words between the women in the Hellcat.

Michelle cradles her belly.

Athena stares at the blacktop.

Not much to talk about.

Just the road ahead.

The destination.

A peaceful death for at least one of em.

At any cost.

ABOUT THE AUTHOR

William Vitka is a writer and journalist with more than ten books under his belt and ten years in the news business. He believes that politicians will be the doom of us all, but at least there's whiskey. His Twitter handle is @vitka and he can be found at facebook.com/VitkaWrites.

BOOK

PERMUTED
PRESS

14

Peter Clines

Padlocked doors. Strange light fixtures. Mutant cockroaches.

There are some odd things about Nate's new apartment. Every room in this old brownstone has a mystery. Mysteries that stretch back over a hundred years. Some of them are in plain sight. Some are behind locked doors. And all together these mysteries could mean the end of Nate and his friends.

Or the end of everything...

PERMUTED
PRESS

THE JOURNAL SERIES
by Deborah D. Moore

After a major crisis rocks the nation, all supply lines are shut down. In the remote Upper Peninsula of Michigan, the small town of Moose Creek and its residents are devastated when they lose power in the middle of a brutal winter, and must struggle alone with one calamity after another.

The Journal series takes the reader head first into the fury that only Mother Nature can dish out.

Michael Clary
THE GUARDIAN | THE REGULATORS | BROKEN

When the dead rise up and take over the city, the Government is forced to close off the borders and abandon the remaining survivors. Fortunately for them, a hero is about to be chosen...a Guardian that will rise up from the ashes to fight against the dead. The series continues with Book Four: *Scratch*.

Emily Goodwin
CONTAGIOUS | DEATHLY CONTAGIOUS

During the Second Great Depression, twenty-four-year-old Orissa Penwell is forced to drop out of college when she is no longer able to pay for classes. Down on her luck, Orissa doesn't think she can sink any lower. She couldn't be more wrong. A virus breaks out across the country, leaving those that are infected crazed, aggressive and very hungry. `

The saga continues in Book Three: *Contagious Chaos* and Book Four: *The Truth is Contagious*.

PERMUTED
PRESS

THE BREADWINNER | Stevie Kopas

The end of the world is not glamorous. In a matter of days the human race was reduced to nothing more than vicious, flesh hungry creatures. There are no heroes here. Only survivors. The trilogy continues with Book Two: *Haven* and Book Three: *All Good Things*.

THE BECOMING | Jessica Meigs

As society rapidly crumbles under the hordes of infected, three people—Ethan Bennett, a Memphis police officer; Cade Alton, his best friend and former IDF sharpshooter; and Brandt Evans, a lieutenant in the US Marines—band together against the oncoming crush of death and terror sweeping across the world. The story continues with Book Two: *Ground Zero*.

THE INFECTION WAR | Craig DiLouie

As the undead awake, a small group of survivors must accept a dangerous mission into the very heart of infection. This edition features two books: *The Infection* and *The Killing Floor*.

OBJECTS OF WRATH | Sean T. Smith

The border between good and evil has always been bloody... Is humanity doomed? After the bombs rain down, the entire world is an open wound; it is in those bleeding years that William Fox becomes a man. After The Fall, nothing is certain. *Objects of Wrath* is the first book in a saga spanning four generations.

PERMUTED
PRESS

A PREPPER'S COOKBOOK
20 Years of Cooking in the Woods
by Deborah D. Moore

In the event of a disaster, it isn't enough to have food. You also have to know what to do with it.

Deborah D. Moore, author of *The Journal* series and a passionate Prepper for over twenty years, gives you step-by-step instructions on making delicious meals from the emergency pantry.

PERMUTED
PRESS